MOGGRIDGE, Donald Edward. John Maynar
190p bibl index 76-21630. 2.95 pa ISBN
Moggridge, a product of Cambridge, probes i
vealing insights into the man and his work. I
Keynes's methodology reflects, in part, his pre
tained a revision of the changing social orc
sirability of management and means-and-ends
tives. Keynes made skillful use of persuasion
major wartime concerns and postwar econom
views on issues involving rationing and taxati
ployment; exchange rate policy; and the Bre
His inspiration evoked in others a revival o
questions he raised; for example, economic ar
lems, long-term questions of economic growth
analysis. Both laymen and students will find t
an eminent economist intent upon improving
kind under reformed capitalism. Readers de
this man should refer to R. F. Harrod's *The*
Keynes (1951).

MODERN MASTERS

ALBERT CAMUS / Conor Cruise O'Brien
FRANTZ FANON / David Caute
HERBERT MARCUSE / Alasdair MacIntyre
CHE GUEVARA / Andrew Sinclair
LUDWIG WITTGENSTEIN / David Pears
GEORGE LUKÁCS / George Lichtheim
NOAM CHOMSKY / John Lyons
JAMES JOYCE / John Gross
MARSHALL MCLUHAN / Jonathan Miller
GEORGE ORWELL / Raymond Williams
SIGMUND FREUD / Richard Wollheim
WILLIAM BUTLER YEATS / Denis Donoghue
WILHELM REICH / Charles Rycroft
MOHANDAS GANDHI / George Woodcock
BERTRAND RUSSELL / A. J. Ayer
NORMAN MAILER / Richard Poirier
V. I. LENIN / Robert Conquest

ALREADY PUBLISHED

EINSTEIN / Jeremy Bernstein
C. G. JUNG / Anthony Storr
D. H. LAWRENCE / Frank Kermode
KARL POPPER / Bryan Magee
SAMUEL BECKETT / A. Alvarez
R. D. LAING / Edgar Z. Friedenberg
MAX WEBER / Donald G. MacRae
MARCEL PROUST / Roger Shattuck
CLAUDE LÉVI-STRAUSS (*Rev. Ed.*) / Edmund Leach
LE CORBUSIER / Stephen Gardiner
ARNOLD SCHOENBERG / Charles Rosen
FRANZ KAFKA / Erich Heller
T. S. ELIOT / Stephen Spender
KARL MARX / David McLellan
JEAN-PAUL SARTRE / Arthur C. Danto
EZRA POUND / Donald Davie
FERDINAND DE SAUSSURE / Jonathan Culler

PENGUIN
MODERN MASTERS

EDITED BY frank kermode

*By Modern Masters we mean the men who have
changed and are changing the life and thought
of our age. The authors of these volumes are
themselves masters, and they have written their
books in the belief that general discussion of
their subjects will henceforth be more informed
and more exciting than ever before.* —F. K.

john maynard keynes

d. e. moggridge

PENGUIN BOOKS

Penguin Books Ltd, Harmondsworth,
Middlesex, England
Penguin Books, 625 Madison Avenue,
New York, New York 10022, U.S.A.
Penguin Books Australia Ltd, Ringwood,
Victoria, Australia
Penguin Books Canada Ltd, 41 Steelcase Road West,
Markham, Ontario, Canada
Penguin Books (N.Z.) Ltd, 182–190 Wairau Road,
Auckland 10, New Zealand

First published in Great Britain by Fontana 1976
Published in Penguin Books 1976

LIBRARY OF CONGRESS CATALOGING IN PUBLICATION DATA

Moggridge, Donald Edward.
John Maynard Keynes.

(Modern masters)
Bibliography: p.
Includes index.
1. Keynes, John Maynard, 1883–1946.
2. Keynesian economics.
HB103.K47M55   330.15'6[B]   76-21630
ISBN 0 14 00.4319 5 (pbk.)

Printed in the United States of America by
Offset Paperback Mfrs., Inc.,
Dallas, Pennsylvania
Set in Linotype Primer

CONTENTS

Acknowledgments ix

Biographical Note xi

Introduction 1

i / Prologue 5

ii / The Economist 20

iii / Glosses on Marshalliana, 1908–25 42

iv / The Period of Transition, 1925–31 72

v / The Years of the *General Theory*, 1931–37 87

vi / The Economist Statesman, 1939–46 116

vii / Conclusion 152

Appendix: A Note on the Standard Presentation of the *General Theory* 171

Short Bibliography 175

Index 183

ACKNOWLEDGMENTS

In writing a book such as this one accumulates many debts to others. I most directly must acknowledge, with the usual disclaimers as to direct responsibility for the errors they didn't catch or the advice I ignored, Austin Robinson, Joan Robinson, Richard Kahn, Mark Blaug, Phyllis Deane, and Donald Winch for their comments on an earlier draft. I should particularly like to thank Susan Howson for her extensive comments on earlier drafts and for her allowing me to make use of her as yet unpublished research on the interwar period which was most particularly useful in writing pages 111–15. Less directly, I must acknowledge the influences that made the first draft possible at all—from Ian Drummond, who ensured that the *General Theory* was the first book I read as an undergraduate economist, through Joan Robinson and Richard Kahn, who acted as my Ph.D. supervisors, and Austin Robinson whose good sense and wise advice has made editing Keynes such a joy and an education, to all those for whom the publication of the Keynes edition has provided opportunities for comment both public and private.

Earlier articles of mine have reappeared in part in places in this book and I should like to thank the following for permission to use them:

The editor of *History of Political Economy* and Duke University Press for permission to use parts of my "From the *Treatise* to the *General Theory: An Exercise in Chronology*," Spring 1973.

The editors of *Oxford Economic Papers* and Oxford University Press for permission to use parts of my article with Susan Howson, "Keynes on Monetary Policy, 1910–1946," July 1974.

The Master of Keynes College, University of Kent, and Macmillan for permission to use parts of my "Keynes: The Economist," in D. E. Moggridge, ed., *Keynes: Aspects of the Man and His Work* (London, 1974).

W. M. Keynes and Cambridge University Press for permission to use parts of my essays "The Influence of Keynes on the Economics of his Time" and "Economic Policy in the Second World War" in Milo Keynes, ed., *Essays on John Maynard Keynes*, (Cambridge, 1975).

For permission to quote from *The Collected Writings of John Maynard Keynes*, I should like to thank the Royal Economic Society, while for unpublished Keynes Papers I should like to thank Lord Kahn. For permission to cite Crown Copyright material I should like to thank the Controller of Her Majesty's Stationery Office.

BIOGRAPHICAL NOTE

1883	Keynes born June 5 at Harvey Road, Cambridge.
1897	Scholarship to Eton.
1902	Enters King's College, Cambridge.
1903	Admitted to the Apostles.
1905–06	Studies economics for Civil Service Examination.
1906	Enters India Office.
1908	Lecturer in economics, University of Cambridge.
1909	Fellow of King's College, Cambridge.
1911	Editor of *Economic Journal*.
1913	*Indian Currency and Finance*.
1913–14	Member, Royal Commission on Indian Finance and Currency.
1915	Joins wartime Treasury.
1919	Principal representative of the Treasury at Paris Peace Conference. In June, resigns from Treasury over the peace treaty. *The Economic Consequences of the Peace* appears in December.
1920	Resigns University lectureship in economics.

1921	*A Treatise on Probability.*
1922	*A Revision of the Treaty.*
1923	*A Tract on Monetary Reform.*
1924	Bursar of King's College, Cambridge.
1925	Marries Lydia Lopokova.
1925, 1928	Visits Russia.
1929–31	Member, Macmillan Committee on Finance and Industry.
1930–39	Member, Economic Advisory Council.
1930	*A Treatise on Money.*
1931	The "Circus" on the *Treatise*, and *Essays in Persuasion.*
1933	*Essays in Biography.*
1936	Opening of Arts Theatre, Cambridge, and *The General Theory of Employment, Interest and Money* published.
1937	Has his first heart attack.
1940	*How to Pay for the War* published. Keynes becomes an adviser to Chancellor of the Exchequer.
1941	Becomes a director of the Bank of England and a trustee of the National Gallery. Visits the United States.
1942	Is named chairman of the Committee for the Encouragement of Music and the Arts (later the Arts Council) and becomes Lord Keynes (Baron Keynes of Tilton).
1944	Attends Bretton Woods Conference and is in on the Washington negotiations on Stage II of Lend Lease.
1945	Goes to Washington for the negotiations on the U.S. Loan to Britain.
1946	Attends the Savannah Conference for the inauguration of International Monetary Fund and World Bank and is appointed to the Order of Merit and made Fellow of the Royal Society. Keynes dies at Tilton, Sussex, on April 21.

JOHN MAYNARD KEYNES

Introduction

It is now thirty years since Easter Sunday in April 1946, when the last of many heart attacks ended Maynard Keynes's life. It is forty years since *The General Theory of Employment, Interest and Money* appeared in British bookshops, priced by the author at five shillings to encourage the widest possible sale, especially among undergraduates.[1] As I write, it is fifty-five years since Keynes sat in a Sussex farmhouse garden composing (and sharing with his friends) *The Economic Consequences of the Peace*.

Despite the passage of the years, interest in

[1] Unlike nearly all modern authors, Keynes had his books published on a commission basis. He advanced the costs of printing, binding, advertising, etc., and paid Macmillan, his publishers, a commission on costs. Hence his ability to influence the pricing decision.

Keynes continues unabated. Editors of economic journals, as well as publishers, continue to receive and publish discussions of what Keynes really meant (or should have meant); negotiators for a revised set of international monetary arrangements, or their research assistants, rummage through his published work or his as yet unpublished World War II memoranda in search of inspiration or justification; politicians, such as ex-President Nixon, still believe that there is political mileage in declaring that they are Keynesians; thousands of students in several disciplines struggle with various aspects of his work. To top it all, finance ministers around the world approach the problems of economic management through an analytical framework which, perhaps for want of a better word, commentators rightly call Keynesian.

In themselves the above would provide reasons enough to justify a reconsideration of his work and ideas. However, Keynes was not merely an economist. His wide range of interests and activities—for example, college bursar, investment trust manager, journal editor; theater builder, Christopher Isherwood and W. H. Auden's London West End theater producer, artists' patron, insurance-company chairman, trustee of the National Gallery, philosopher and bibliophile—plus his urge to action rather than inaction, meant that he affected modern British life in other ways. Members of, and visitors to, his Cambridge College, King's, continue to benefit from his successful financial stewardship as bursar, not to mention his bequest. Cambridge residents and visitors enjoy the arts in the theater he founded, nursed to financial viability, and presented to the City and University. Others enjoy the Royal Ballet, successor to the Camargo Society and the Vic-Wells Ballet, both of which benefited from his active interest; enjoy the British national collection of modern French paintings started by Keynes as a Treasury official supplying the French with sterling in 1918; or experience the results of the work of the Arts Council, whose founding absorbed some of Keynes's scarce energy during World War II.

Who was this economist, whose influence, directly or indirectly, affects so many lives—whom many praise and not a few condemn? What were his intellectual origins, his characteristic modes of thought, his beliefs, his ideas? In the pages that follow I hope to provide something of the flavor of the man, of his work, of his approach to the problems of his age, and of his influence on our own.

Prologue

i

Keynes was a product of Victorian and Edwardian England. This fact helps to explain many of his characteristic attitudes and habits of thought. Surely in that age one could assume that prices and interest rates were relatively stable: 1914 saw prices 11 per cent below the level of fifty years earlier, and the range of fluctuation of long-term interest rates over the same period was between 2.5 and 3.4 per cent. Again, one might be forgiven for normally assuming that the government of Britain was in the hands of an intellectual elite: voters could choose between H. H. Asquith and A. J. Balfour as to who would exercise responsibility for a small civil service dominated by a meritocracy recruited by competitive examination in subjects that only Oxford and Cambridge seemed able to teach.

Keynes's family background was Victorian academia. His father, John Neville Keynes, was a noted philosopher, economist, and academic administrator, whose *Formal Logic* and *Scope and Method of Political Economy* remain minor classics. His mother, Florence Ada, an early graduate of Newnham College, Cambridge, was active in Cambridge local affairs, the City's first woman councilor and eventually its mayor. His childhood at Harvey Road as the eldest of three children appears to have been happy and conventional. His education was also conventional—a governess, a local kindergarten and preparatory school, a satisfactory, but undistinguished scholarship to Eton, and a more distinguished open scholarship in classics and mathematics to King's College, Cambridge. During his period at Eton, where he was noted for his new white tie every day and a fresh boutonniere every morning during his last eighteen months, Keynes's interests broadened considerably, so that, by the time he came up to King's to read mathematics in October 1902, he was bound to take part in a wide variety of political, literary, and other activities. Of these, perhaps the most important to his development was membership in the group eventually known as Bloomsbury.

Keynes became involved toward the end of his first term in Cambridge, after an inspection visit from Leonard Woolf and Lytton Strachey, two of Bloomsbury's Cambridge "founder members." As a result of the visit, in February 1903, he joined the Apostles, a small, secret Cambridge society of dons, former undergraduates, and undergraduates originally formed in the 1820s by F. D. Maurice. Several Apostles would become prominent in the Bloomsbury group. Among the older active members were C. P. Sanger, Desmond MacCarthy, Bertrand Russell, and G. Lowes Dickinson. Among the younger were Strachey, Woolf, Saxon Sidney-Turner,

E. M. Forster, and H. O. Meredith. The paramount older
influence in the society, with its respect for truth and
nothing else, was G. E. Moore, the philosopher, whose
Principia Ethica appeared in the autumn of 1903.

At the time Keynes became an Apostle, its members
were in the process of taking certain presuppositions of
nineteenth-century rationalism further afield. Whereas,
"in Victorian England . . . the apostles of progress . . .
swept their churches clean of sacraments, altars, priests
and pulpits, leaving nothing save a bare structure of
ethical assertions,"[1] their personal relations were characterized by superstition, cant, and traditionalism. The
Apostles of the time, and later Bloomsbury, turned with
gusto to these personal relationships and morality. Some
of their attitudes come out clearly in Keynes's comments
to a friend from Eton, then at Oxford, on the auto-
biographical *Memoir* by Henry Sidgwick, a Cambridge
philosopher, former Apostle, freethinker, and economist,
with whom Keynes had played golf as a young man and
the proofs of whose posthumous edition of *Principles
of Political Economy* had been Keynes's to correct just
before he came up to King's:

> Have you read Sidgwick's life? It seems to be the sub-
> ject of conversation now. Very interesting and depress-
> ing, and, the first part particularly, very important as
> an historical document dealing with the mind of the
> period. Really—but you must read it yourself. He
> never did anything but wonder whether Christianity
> was true and prove that it wasn't and hope that it was.
> He even learnt Arabic [*sic*] in order to read Genesis
> in the original, not trusting the authorised translators,
> which does seem a little sceptical. . . .
> I wonder what he would have thought of us; and I
> wonder what we think of him. And then his con-
> science—incredible. There is no doubt about his moral

goodness. And yet it is all so dreadfully depressing—
no intimacy, no clear-cut crisp boldness. Oh, I suppose
he was intimate but he didn't seem to have anything
to be intimate about except his religious doubts. And
he really ought to have got over that a little sooner;
because he knew that the thing wasn't true perfectly
well from the beginning. The last part is all about
ghosts and Mr. Balfour. I have never found so dull a
book so absorbing.[2]

In this process of re-examining personal relationships
and morality, Moore's *Principia Ethica* view that "good"
is an attribute, the meaning of which is indefinable, and
that, therefore, decisions as to what is "good" depend
on the circumstances of the particular case, provided
the Apostles with a considerable sense of liberation and
fairly complete license to examine matters anew. In
addition, Moore's emphasis that greatest value resides in
certain states of mind—the contemplation of beauty,
love, and truth—meant that the re-examination would
center primarily on personal morality. Keynes himself
summarized the result in a paper to the Bloomsbury
memoir club in 1938:

The influence was not only overwhelming; . . . it was
exciting, exhilarating, the beginning of a renaissance,
the opening of a new heaven on a new earth, we were
the forerunners of a new dispensation, we were not
afraid of anything. . . .

Now what we got from Moore was by no means
entirely what he offered us. He had one foot on the
threshold of the new heaven, but the other foot in
Sidgwick and the Benthamite calculus and the general
rules of correct behaviour. There was one chapter in
the *Principia* of which we took not the slightest
notice. We accepted Moore's religion, so to speak, and

[2] Letter dated March 27, 1906. (All spelling, punctuation,
and italization are as in the originals unless otherwise noted.)

discarded his morals. Indeed, in our opinion, one of the greatest advantages of his religion was that it made morals unnecessary—meaning by "religion" one's attitude towards oneself and the ultimate and by "morals" one's attitude towards the outside world and the intermediate. . . .

Nothing mattered except states of mind, our own and other people's of course, but chiefly our own. These states of mind were not associated with action or achievement or with consequences. They consisted in timeless, passionate states of contemplation and communion, largely unattached to "before" and "after." Their value depended, in accordance with the principle of organic unity, on the state of affairs as a whole which could not be usefully analysed into parts. For example, the value of the state of mind of being in love did not merely depend on the nature of one's own emotions, but also on the worth of their object and on the reciprocity and nature of the object's emotions; but it did not depend, if I remember rightly, or did not depend much, on what happened, of how one felt about it, a year later. . . . The appropriate subjects of passionate contemplation and communion were a beloved person, beauty and truth, and one's prime objectives in life were love, the creation and enjoyment of aesthetic experience and the pursuit of knowledge. Of these love came a long way first. . . .

Our religion closely followed the English puritan tradition of being chiefly concerned with the salvation of our own souls. The divine resided within a closed circle. There was not a very intimate connection between "being good" and "doing good"; and we had a feeling that there was some risk that in practice the latter might interfere with the former. . . .

But we set on one side, not only that part of Moore's fifth chapter on "Ethics in Relation to Conduct" which dealt with the obligation so to act as to produce by causal connection the most probable maximum of eventual good through the whole procession of future ages . . . but also the part which discussed the duty of the individual to obey general rules. We entirely repudiated a personal liability on us to obey general rules. We claimed the right to judge every individual case on its merits, and the wisdom, experience and self-control to do so successfully. This was a very important part of our faith, violently and aggressively held, and for the outer world it was our most obvious and dangerous characteristic. We repudiated entirely customary morals, conventions and traditional wisdom. We were, that is to say, in the strict sense of the term, immoralists. The consequences of being found out had, of course, to be considered for what they were worth. But we recognised no moral obligation on us, no inner sanction, to conform or obey. Before heaven we claimed to be our own judge in our own case. . . .

We were among the last of the Utopians, or meliorists as they are sometimes called, who believe in a continuing moral progress by virtue of which the human race already consists of reliable, rational, decent people, influenced by truth and objective standards, who can be safely released from the outward restraints of convention and traditional standards and inflexible rules of conduct, and left, from now onwards, to their own sensible devices, pure motives and reliable intuitions of the good.[3]

This ethic, which to some extent Keynes was questioning in his 1938 memoir, with its traces of "philosopher kingship" behind it, stood at the center of the Apostles and Bloomsbury as they got on with the business of living. Although they were, by modern standards, restrained in language and romantic in their attachments, it is not surprising that those involved left behind much of the personal morality of the Victorians. Cer-

[3] "My Early Beliefs," *Collected Writings of John Maynard Keynes* (hereafter cited in the text as JMK) X, 435–47.

tainly, under Keynes's and Strachey's influence, one of
the sporadic traditions of the Apostles, "that of the
'higher sodomy,' a sort of ideological homosexuality,
which manifested itself more in words than in deeds,"[4]
returned with some shift in emphasis toward the deed.
But there was little guilt and firm friendships endured,
as passions and tastes changed over the years. Moreover, Bloomsbury's inclusion of women on an equal
footing made it remarkable for its age—and, in many
respects, for our own.

The emphasis on personal standards of morality and
judgment and respect for personal integrity come out
clearly in many individual acts of Keynes, but to our age
perhaps the most interesting relate to the period of
World War I. One concerns Ferenc Bekassy, a Hun-
garian poet associated with Bloomsbury. Just before the
outbreak of war, he wished to return home to fight
against Russia, but, owing to the closure of the banks
during the war-related financial crisis, he could not get
money to enable him to leave England. Keynes, after
trying every argument to persuade him not to go, raised
the money, and Bekassy left the day before war was
declared. He died on active service. When questioned
about his behavior by David Garnett, Keynes replied
that it was not the part of a friend to impose his views
by force or by refusal to help. When Garnett asked him
then if he would restrain a friend contemplating suicide
or lend him money for poison, "Maynard replied that
in certain circumstances he would lend him the money
—if it was a free choice, made by a sane man after due
reflection, for compelling causes."[5]

A second example concerned conscription. Throughout the autumn of 1915 there had been a growing

---

[4] P. Levy, "The Bloomsbury Group," in M. Keynes, ed., *Essays on John Maynard Keynes*, p. 64.
[5] D. Garnett, *The Golden Echo* (New York, 1954), p. 271.

demand for compulsory military service. Lord Derby's campaign to get men of military age to attest their willingness to enlist failed to produce a sufficient number of volunteers, and the government put through the Military Service Act at the end of January 1916, by which all men between eighteen and forty-one who were unmarried or widowers without dependent children were "deemed . . . to have duly enlisted." Many of Keynes's friends—Lytton and James Strachey, Duncan Grant, Gerald Shove, Bertrand Russell, David Garnett—were pacifists. Keynes's own attitude had been closest to that of Sir John Simon, who resigned from the cabinet over the issue, believing that the state did not have the right to take over this individual decision.[6] With the change in the law—against which he had worked through letters to the press and suggestions of amendments to a sympathetic Member of Parliament—Keynes turned his efforts to attesting to the virtue and truthfulness of his friends' conscientious objections and to considering his own personal duty.

Technically, he was not required to do anything, for as a civil servant in the Treasury he was exempt from the Act. However, he did seriously consider resigning his post. In the end, although already exempt, he applied to his local tribunal for exemption on grounds of conscientious objection. He was unable to appear in person before the tribunal, owing to official business, and left it to decide his case on the basis of the following note:

> I claim complete exemption because I have a conscientious objection to surrendering my liberty of judgment on so vital a question as undertaking military service. I do not say that there are not conceivable circumstances in which I should voluntarily offer

[6] Keynes also opposed conscription on more prosaic economic grounds; see *JMK*, XVI, 110–15, 157–61.

myself for military service. But after having regard to the actually existing circumstances, I am certain that it is not my duty to offer myself; and I solemnly assert to the Tribunal that my objection to submit to authority in this matter is truly conscientious. I am not prepared on such an issue as this to surrender my right of decision, as to what is or is not my duty, to any other person, and I should think it morally wrong to do so.

The tribunal behaved sensibly in the circumstances, evading the issue raised by Keynes by dismissing his application as unnecessary, given his previous exemption. This incident gives some indication of the strains that Bloomsbury beliefs put on a member faced with the choices of total war. The members of the circle themselves did not make Keynes's position during the war easier, for their general pacifism put great strains on one so close to the center of wartime financial management. Nevertheless, Keynes remained his own man.[7] In the end, he made his own more effective protest against official policy in 1919, with his resignation from the Treasury and his *Economic Consequences of the Peace*.

The influence of Bloomsbury, its rationalism, its general optimism, and its emphasis on the importance of individuals, left other marks on Keynes, as we shall see in considering his work as an economist, his view of the political process, and his understanding of the good society.

---

[7] On the issue of Keynes's conscientious objection, see the exchange between Elizabeth Johnson and Sir Roy Harrod in the *Economic Journal* of March 1960. On the pressures of Bloomsbury, see, for example, D. Garnett, *The Flowers of the Forest*, (New York, 1956), pp. 148–50; P. Levy, *op. cit.*, pp. 66–70.

When graduated in 1905 it was far from clear that he would be an economist. His degree in mathematics, twelfth in first-class honors, was respectable, especially given the relatively little work he had put into it, but it was not of a standard to suggest further research in the area, even if Keynes's first love had been mathematics. Some, such as G. M. Trevelyan, suggested the bar and politics; others suggested he spend another year and do another Tripos in moral sciences or economics. Keynes, however, decided to prepare for the Civil Service examinations to be held in August 1906. Part of this preparation involved economics, and one finds Keynes attending Alfred Marshall's lectures and preparing essays for the Professor, who began to try to persuade him to become a professional economist. But as his contemporaries had graduated, Keynes seems to have been determined to get out of Cambridge, which he found "deadening." He persisted with the Civil Service, coming second of 104 candidates in the examinations. Somewhat surprisingly, his examiners judged that his worst papers were in mathematics and economics.

As was then the custom, after the examination results appeared, the authorities announced the list of vacancies. There was only one at the Treasury that year, and when O. E. Niemeyer, as the top candidate, took that post after some hesitation, Keynes entered the India Office's Military Department. However, before he entered the Civil Service, he had started work on a prize fellowship dissertation for King's on probability theory.[8] Initially, his work in the Military Department proved so undemanding that he got into the habit of working on his dissertation during office hours, but on his transfer to the Revenue, Statistics and Commerce Department,

[8] A prize fellowship could be held concurrently with a Civil Service post and imposed no Cambridge residence requirements.

he found the work more interesting and demanding. However, he declined a resident clerkship in the India Office to leave time for his dissertation and to allow him the independence to use his out-of-office time as he wished.

The dissertation did not gain him a fellowship in 1908, but it was successful the following year, and after his election, Keynes read even more widely in the subject and greatly enlarged the dissertation for publication. In fact, between 1906 and 1911 he devoted most of his intellectual energy to the theory of probability, before he set his book aside, owing to other commitments, returning to it only during 1920 to make final revisions prior to its eventual publication in 1921.

Keynes's *A Treatise on Probability* was the first systematic work on the logical foundations of probability in English for fifty-five years.[9] Unlike Keynes's other work, it is notable not only for its substantive theory, which has been the basis for subsequent work by philosophers in Cambridge and elsewhere, but also for its extensive discussion of the literature of the subject. In *Probability*, Keynes was concerned with the problem of how intuitive knowledge could form the basis for rational belief which fell short of knowledge itself. In dealing with this problem, he defined probability as a logical relationship between propositions similar to but weaker than logical consequence: "We are claiming, in fact, to cognise correctly a logical connection between one set of propositions which we call our evidence and which we suppose ourselves to know, and another set which we

[9] In the theory of probability, as elsewhere, there are two main schools, the scientific (which attempts to consider probability as a science of the same order as geometry or theoretical mechanics) and the logical (which treats probability as a branch of logic concerned with the logical relationships between propositions).

call our conclusions, and to which we attach more or less weight according to the grounds supplied by the first. . . . It is not straining the use of words to speak of this as the relation of probability" (*JMK*, VIII, 6).

In arguing out the implications of this view, Keynes insisted that most probability relationships were not measurable and that many pairs of relationships were incommensurable. Thus, unlike his successors in the logical school, he believed that it was impossible to arrange such relations in a simple linear order running between certainty of truth and certainty of falsehood. In addition, Keynes went further than his successors have been prepared to go in supposing that his logical interpretation of probability applied to every field in which the term found use, including empirical scientific statements, which his successors have left to the statisticians working in a different tradition. Nevertheless, Keynes's discussion of statistical inference is of interest to those attempting to understand his reactions to the early econometric work of economists such as Jan Tinbergen.[10] Finally, Keynes's successors among the logical school would approach differently the problem of dealing with probability in the sense of reasonable partial belief. As R. B. Braithwaite the author of the editorial foreword to the edition of *Probability* in Keynes's *Collected Writings* puts it:

[10] Thus the objections in his 1939 review of Tinbergen's *Statistical Testing of Business Cycle Theories: A Method and Its Application to Investment Activity* (*JMK*, XIV, 306–20) again and again echo points raised in Book V of *Probability*. The undergraduate teaching of statistics and econometrics today stands on the Nyman-Pearson theory of "objective" probability. For an indication of how this relates to Keynes's "subjective" theory in the context of many issues in modern economics the reader should consult the fascinating and suggestive book by G. L. S. Shackle, *Epistemics and Economics: A Critique of Economic Doctrines*, esp. Book VI.

Keynes takes a logical probability-relationship between two propositions as fundamental to his explanation of rational partial belief, and he maintains that in suitable cases this relationship can be perceived, directly recognised, intuited. . . . But most present-day logicians would be chary of using such verbs as "perceive" to describe knowledge of logical-consequence relationships. . . .

Consequently many of those today who think about the logic of partial belief would not start with a probability relationship and take a degree of belief as being justified by knowledge that a probability relation holds, but would start with a degree of belief and consider what conditions this must satisfy in order to be regarded as one which a rational man would have under given circumstances. To start this way requires a notion of degrees of belief which is independent of considerations of rationality. (*JMK*, VIII, xix–xx)

This leads on to the notion of betting quotients developed out of the work of F. P. Ramsey (a close friend of Keynes's in the 1920s before his unfortunate death at twenty-seven) and of Bruno de Finetti, along which the line of debate revived by Keynes continues unabated.

Given that *Probability* was Keynes's main intellectual interest over such a long period, I must naturally ask why he became an economist, and one with such strong applied interests at that. Certainly before his return to Cambridge in 1908—and even afterward—his friends never thought he would become a professional economist. As late as the winter of 1907–08, in writing to A. C. Pigou, who was about to succeed Marshall as Professor of Political Economy, Keynes said that if he returned to Cambridge his field of study would be logic and statistical theory. Nevertheless, in June 1908 he gave up his India Office post to return to Cambridge (without a college fellowship) at the invitation of Pigou, who, following Marshall's practice, paid two lecturers £100 a year out of his own pocket to fill out the lecturing for the recently founded economic tripos.[11]

Keynes had enjoyed economics when first exposed to it in a formal way—after years of informal exposure at home—while preparing for the civil-service examination in 1905–06. Thus he wrote to Lytton Strachey in November 1905, "I find Economics increasingly satisfactory, and I think I am rather good at it. I want to manage a railway or organize a Trust. . . . It is so easy and fascinating to master the principles of these things." That he was "rather good at it" is clear from Marshall's comments on his work and his "pestering" of Keynes to become a professional economist. However, at that time, Marshall was not persuasive, perhaps partially because of his strong taint of Victorianism and partially because at that stage Keynes had had enough of Cambridge. But by 1908 the India Office and its way of life, on experience, did not appeal as much to Keynes as the prospect of "scientific and theoretical work" and the way of life that Cambridge offered. Moreover, Keynes's India Office work had given him some experience of applied economics and an initial

[11] In addition to the £100 from Pigou, Keynes's father promised him £100 per annum and there was the prospect of fees from lectures and supervisions. If Keynes was successful with his *Probability* and obtained a fellowship at King's, his income would rise by another £120. Keynes's biographer, Sir Roy Harrod, implies that in taking this certain basic income plus outside fees in place of his India Office salary of just over £200 per annum Keynes was taking quite a risk. However, in an age when average annual incomes from employment stood at just over £53 and the average annual earnings of those on salaries was £130, £200 was no small sum. If Keynes were to be paid in 1974 at the same ratio to average annual incomes from employment, his £200 would stand at £8215 before taxes.

In fact, in the first full tax year after he left the India Office, Keynes reckoned his income from all sources at £780.

basis for lecturing and research, as his publications in economics during the next five years were to indicate. Like Marshall, Keynes made the transition from mathematician to economist through philosophy, although in Keynes's case the element of drifting into the subject was probably stronger than his initial commitment. Certainly, philosophy never lost its appeal, as is shown by his subsequent working up of *Probability* for publication and his enjoyment of philosophical speculation with his own and the subsequent generations of Cambridge philosophers.

The Economist

Before examining the development of Keynes's economic ideas between the time of his return to Cambridge and his death, one should try to get inside the man and the mind behind the ideas in question—one must become aware of his habits of thought, his methods of working, his views as to the nature of economic inquiry, and the like. Fortunately, although Keynes did not leave behind an autobiography or a treatise on the nature of economic inquiry, his drafts, correspondence, comments on the work of others, and asides provide one with enough clues to begin to catch the flavor of the economist.

Perhaps the best starting point is to look again at the intellectual environment from which Keynes emerged—at Cambridge. There was a distinctive characteristic in the work of the founding generation of modern Cambridge

economics which many of its successors share. Alfred
Marshall, A. C. Pigou, Henry Sidgwick, and Neville
Keynes in their work as a whole regarded economics as
a moral science. Although they accepted a theoretical
distinction between positive and normative arguments,
they saw that the two were closely intermingled in practice. Thus Pigou characterized Marshall's development:
"Starting out then with the view that economic science
is chiefly valuable, neither as an intellectual gymnastic
nor even as a means of winning truths for its own sake,
but as a handmaid of ethics and a servant of practice,
Marshall resolutely set himself to mould his work along
lines conforming to his ideal."[1] Or, as Keynes put it to
Harrod in 1938, during the discussion of the latter's
presidential address to the Royal Economic Society,
"Scope and Method of Economics"—and of Jan Tinbergen's *Statistical Testing of Business Cycle Theories:*

It seems to me that economics is a branch of logic, a
way of thinking; and that you do not repel sufficiently
firmly attempts . . . to turn it into a pseudo-natural
science. . . .

Economics is a science of thinking in terms of
models joined to the art of choosing models which are
relevant to the contemporary world. It is compelled
to be this, because, unlike the typical natural science,
the material to which it is applied is, in too many
respects, not homogeneous through time. The object
of a model is to segregate the semi-permanent or relatively constant factors from those which are transitory
or fluctuating so as to develop a logical way of thinking about the latter. . . .

Good economists are scarce because the gift for
using "vigilant observation" to choose good models,
although it does not require a highly specialised intellectual technique, appears to be a very rare one.

[1] A.C. Pigou, ed., *Memorials of Alfred Marshall* (London,
1925), p. 84.

In the second place, as against Robbins,[2] economics is essentially a moral science and not a natural science. That is to say, it employs introspection and judgements of value. . . .

I also want to emphasise strongly the point about economics being a moral science. I mentioned before that it deals with introspection and with values. I might have added that it deals with motives, expectations, psychological uncertainties. One has to be constantly on one's guard against treating the material as constant and homogeneous. It is as though the fall of the apple to the ground depended on the apple's motives, on whether it is worthwhile falling to the ground, and whether the ground wants the apple to fall, and on mistaken calculations on the part of the apple as to how far it was from the centre of the earth. (*JMK*, XIV, 296–97, 300)

One aspect of the ethical nature of Cambridge economics, both in Marshall's day and later, was a strong commitment to certain practical social ends. Keynes noted it clearly of Marshall in his charming obituary notice (*JMK*, X, 161–231). Pigou observed the same tendencies in Keynes, in terms surprisingly similar to his comment on Marshall twenty-four years earlier.

Both [Keynes and Marshall] were alike in their single-minded search for truth and also in their desire that the study of Economics should serve, not as a mere intellectual gymnastic, but directly, or at least indirectly, for the forwarding of human welfare. . . . In his *General Theory* there are some, as I think, unwarranted strictures on parts of Marshall's *Principles*. But that in no wise meant that he had ceased to be a firm disciple of the "Master."[3]

[2] L. C. Robbins, *The Nature and Significance of Economic Science* (London, 1932), an extremely influential book in the thinking of economists in the 1930s.
[3] A. C. Pigou, "The Economist," in *John Maynard Keynes 1883–1946* (Cambridge, 1949), p. 21.

Other contemporaries of Keynes also remarked repeatedly on Keynes's extremely practical bent as an economist: his dislike of theory for theory's sake, his almost complete absorption in questions of policy. It was this characteristic that lay behind his choice of emphasis in handling theoretical problems in the *General Theory*. As he told J. R. Hicks in June 1935: "I deliberately refrain in my forthcoming book from pursuing anything very far, my object being to press home as forcibly as possible certain fundamental opinions—and no more." In fact, Keynes's ideal economist was in many respects a practical, if right thinking, technician—a dentist, to borrow one of his phrases. In his own work as an economist, Keynes might almost find himself classified as an extraordinary civil servant, using traditional modes of analysis until they broke down and then proceeding to fashion new tools to fill in the gaps—little more. Keynes saw the economist as providing an essential element in the possibility of civilization—a role that echoed Marshall's hopes in his inaugural lecture:

> It will be my most cherished ambition . . . to increase the numbers of those, whom Cambridge, the great mother of strong men, sends out into the world with cool heads but warm hearts, willing to give some at least of their best powers to grappling with the social suffering around them; resolved not to rest content till they have done what in them lies to discover how far it is possible to open up all the material means of a refined and noble life.[4]

This practicality colored all of Keynes's working life as an economist. It came out clearly in his comments on the work of others—as a reader of manuscripts for publishers, editor of the *Economic Journal*, unofficial civil servant, or general reader. A typical reply to a possible *Journal* contributor, dated April 1944, runs: "I

[4] Pigou, ed., *Memorials of Alfred Marshall*, p. 174.

do not doubt that a serious problem will arise when we have a combination of collective bargaining and full employment. But I am not sure how much light the analytical [economic] method you apply can throw on this essentially political problem." Again, in October 1944, when asked to comment on the idea of "functional finance"—a theoretical attempt to devise a general rule for countercyclical budgetary policy to maintain full employment—he remarked that "functional finance is an idea and not a policy; part of one's apparatus of thought but not, except highly diluted under a considerable clothing of qualification, an apparatus of action. Economist have to be very careful, I think, to distinguish the two." Useful words to consider again after a period when economists have provided us with ideas masquerading as policy in such forms as the Phillips Curve "explaining" the relation between money wage claims and unemployment.

This leads us on to another characteristic of Keynes, one not unexpected in the author of *A Treatise on Probability*. For Keynes, more than most, approached all problems with a mind that attempted to get to the fundamental basis of an argument or a system of ideas. As one Treasury economist-colleague of the World War II period put it in a letter:

I would say that what dominated his approach to any matter was a philosophy—a habit of mind. He was always ready and eager to make the best possible synthesis of the available data, thence to carry this reasoning where it might lead him and to *offer* (repeat offer) conclusions. But unlike many, he never forgot the fundamental importance of premises and the invalidity of good reasoning on incomplete premises (Propn. 2.21 of [Russell's and Whitehead's] *Principia Mathematica* refers). So while it was usually impossible to attack his reasoning, he was always ready and willing to revise his conclusions if his premises were attacked and could be shown to be wrong or imperfect. He could be pretty difficult in resisting attack, but if it succeeded—never mind whether from the office boy, or the office cat for that matter—he had the tremendous capacity of always being willing to start afresh and re-synthesise. . . . So the continuing value, as it seemed to me, of so much of his work in that time was in provoking critical examination and analysis of the facts of the situation —the premises.

It was Keynes's seriousness concerning assumptions and premises that underlay much of the purpose of the *General Theory*. There, Keynes attacked his "classical" contemporaries, not because they disagreed with him on policy proposals in connection with the slump—in fact, many of them wrote joint letters to *The Times* with him and sat on committees exhibiting a fair degree of unanimity in their reports—but because he believed that their policy recommendations were inconsistent with the premises of the theory they used to explain the situation. One must remember that he singled out Professor L. C. Robbins, the economist with whom he disagreed perhaps most on policy throughout the 1930s, as almost alone among his contemporaries as one whose "practical recommendations belong . . . to the same system as his theory" (*JMK*, VII, 20n). Thus in 1937, after the publication of Pigou's *Socialism versus Capitalism*, Keynes could write to Richard Kahn: "Many thanks for sending me a copy of the Prof's new book. As in the case of Dennis [Robertson], when it comes to practice, there is really extremely little between us. Why do they insist on maintaining theories from which their own practical conclusions cannot possibly follow? It is a sort of Society for the Preservation of Ancient Monuments" (*JMK*, XIV, 259). In the 1930s Keynes believed that this inconsistency between premises and conclusions was a source of weakness in the economists' attempts to influence policy. For, on occasion, it led to unnecessary and unhelpful public controversy that obscured the issues at stake. Thus he attempted to get his professional colleagues to reconsider their premises. Whether he fully succeeded is a subject for discussion in a later chapter.

With a knowledge of this aspect of his approach to problems one can understand more fully Keynes's many contributions to public and professional discussion. In *The Economic Consequences of the Peace* (1919) he was questioning the assumptions concerning the nature of the European economic system implicit in the peace treaties following World War I. Similarly, in *The Economic Consequences of Mr. Churchill* (1925) he questioned the authorities' assumptions concerning the international economic position of Britain in 1925 and the mechanism of adjustment to a higher exchange rate following their decision to return to the gold standard at what he believed was an overvalued rate. Again, in his discussion of the early econometric work of economists such as Tinbergen, Keynes, who was not unsympathetic to such work and was at the time founding the Cambridge Department of Applied Economics, turned—as was natural for both Keynes the economist and Keynes the author of *A Treatise on Probability*—to the assumptions and premises of the methodology involved.[5] In fact, perhaps Keynes's great influence as

---

[5] Keynes undertook the review of Tinbergen's work at the request of his assistant editor on the *Economic Journal*, after he had privately commented on an early draft for the League of Nations, which had sponsored the work. When he submitted the review, he admitted to his assistant editor that the work might not be within his competence and his review might be a waste of time. It certainly made some formal mistakes in understanding Tinbergen's detailed method, but the questioning of assumptions was most characteristic.

a molder of professional economic and public opinion came from his efforts to set out clearly the implicit assumptions of others for scrutiny rather than to quibble over details.

Despite Keynes's emphasis on the premises of arguments and his care in the development of many of his own ideas—exemplified by the definitional chapters of his *General Theory* which took an immense (indeed, inordinate) amount of his time during 1934–35—it would be very misleading to leave the reader with the picture of a remorseless logician. For Keynes was the most intuitive of men. Moreover, in a series of what must certainly be introspective passages, he recognized the role of intuition in the work of others in the course of his biographical essays on Newton, Malthus, and Marshall (*JMK*, X). The Marshall passage, written in 1924 while he was wrestling with the early drafts of what became *A Treatise on Money* (1930), is perhaps the most useful in this connection:

> But it was an essential truth to which he held firmly that those individuals who are endowed with a special genius for the subject of economics and have a powerful economic intuition will often be more right in their conclusions and implicit presumptions than in their explanations and explicit statements. That is to say, their intuitions will be in advance of their analysis and their terminology. Great respect, therefore, is due to their general scheme of thought, and it is a poor thing to pester their memories with criticism which is purely verbal. (*JMK*, X, 211*n*)

The intuitive nature of Keynes's thought processes comes out clearly at many points in Keynes's work as an economist. Occasionally, in his discussions with possible contributors to the *Economic Journal*, he might make the nature of his thought process explicit and write, "You have not expressed it in a way in which I am able to bring my intuition to bear clearly." Similarly, in the development of his *General Theory* one can see from students' lecture notes, correspondence, and drafts that Keynes had intuitively grasped most of the essentials of his system as early as 1932. However, if there was no doubt about the truth, there was considerable trouble over the proof, and it took another three years of redrafting and discussion to clothe that intuition in what he regarded as a technically adequate form for the purposes at hand. With Keynes intuition represented an early, but essential, stage in the act of creation. Very hard, systematic work then went into developing the scheme of thought for the consumption and persuasion of the world at large.

Believing that intuition normally ran a little way ahead of formal analysis, Keynes naturally expected a considerable amount from his readers. He made his position most clear in a 1934 draft preface for the *General Theory*:

When we write economic theory, we write in a quasi-formal style; and there can be no doubt, in spite of the disadvantages, that this is our best available means of conveying our thoughts to one another. But when an economist writes in a quasi-formal style . . . he never states all his premises and his definitions are not perfectly clear-cut. He never mentions all the qualifications necessary to his conclusions. He has no means of stating, once and for all, the precise level of abstraction on which he is moving, and he does not move on the same level all the time. It is, I think, of the nature of economic exposition that it gives, not a complete statement . . . but a sample statement . . . intended to suggest to the reader the whole bundle of associated ideas, so that, if he catches the bundle, he will not be the least confused or impeded by the technical incompleteness of the mere words. . . .
This means, on the one hand, that an economic

writer requires from his reader much goodwill and intelligence and a large measure of co-operation; and, on the other hand, that there are a thousand futile, yet verbally legitimate, objections which an objector can raise. In economics you cannot *convict* your opponent of error—you can only *convince* him of it. And, even if you are right, you cannot convince him, if there is a defect in your own powers of persuasion and exposition or if his head is already so filled with contrary notions that he cannot catch the clues to your thought which you are trying to throw to him. (*JMK*, XIII, 469–70)

It was this point of view, a result of Keynes's own habits of thought and work, that explains his unusually fierce reactions to criticism, as on the occasion of Professor F. A. Hayek's review of his *Treatise on Money*. In replying to it, Keynes turned on Hayek's most recent book as follows:

The reader will perceive that I have been drifting into a review of Dr. Hayek's *Prices and Production*. And this being so, I should like, if the editor will allow me, to consider this book a little further. The book, as it stands, seems to me to be one of the most frightful muddles that I have ever read, with scarcely a sound proposition in it beginning with page 45, and yet it remains a book of some interest, which is likely to leave its mark on the mind of the reader. It is an extraordinary example of how, starting with a mistake, a remorseless logician can end up in Bedlam. Yet Dr. Hayek has seen a vision, and though when he woke up he has made a nonsense of his story by giving the wrong names to the objects which occur in it, his Khubla [*sic*] Khan is not without inspiration and must set the reader thinking with the germs of an idea in his head. (*JMK*, XIII, 252)

When one looks at Keynes's copy of Hayek's review, the most heavily annotated article in the surviving copies of his journals, one finds he wrote at the end: "Hayek has not read my book with that measure of 'goodwill' which an author is entitled to expect of a reader. Until he does so, he will not know what I mean or whether I am right." Perhaps a similar reaction to what he believed to be unsympathetic criticism helped to mar (from Keynes's side) the once pleasant and fruitful relationship between Keynes and D. H. Robertson in the course of the 1930s.

One final consequence of Keynes's habits of thought and working is his use of "the Cambridge didactic style" in presenting his arguments. This was another way in which his writings often followed those of Marshall. When either Keynes or Marshall faced a subtle, but complex problem in pursuing an argument, he would use all the resources at his command to solve it. However, having solved it, rather than taking the reader through the analytical process he had completed, he would provide him with a strategic short cut which would save the reader from considering the problem, yet leave the author's flank protected against possible professional criticism. As Keynes described Marshall's use of the method:

> The lack of emphasis and of strong light and shade, the sedulous rubbing away of rough edges and salients and projections, until what is most novel can appear as trite, allows the reader to pass too easily through. . . . The difficulties are concealed; the most ticklish problems are solved in footnotes; a pregnant and original judgment is dressed up as a platitude. . . . It needs much study and independent thought on the reader's own part before he can know the half of what is contained in the concealed crevices of that rounded globe of knowledge which is Marshall's *Principles of Economics*. (JMK, X, 212)

Keynes himself, being more willing to "fling pamphlets to the wind" and "trust in the efficacy of the co-operation of many minds," was, perhaps, less of a master of the "style" than Marshall, but it is always there to trap the unwary in his more formal writings.

So far, I have concentrated on Keynes's mental processes—his habits of thought and his characteristic methods of attacking problems. However, one cannot understand Keynes's work completely without some reference to his views on how government policies were made in Britain and on the appropriate types of policy. With his emphasis on the practical, his almost desperate desire to influence policy, and his numerous attempts to persuade policy-makers (both privately and publicly), they are vital for an appreciation of his work as an economist.

As a day-to-day working economist, looking out on the world of his age, Keynes was very much the rationalist —perhaps too much so. His career represented a constant campaign bristling with moral indignation at the harm perpetrated by "madmen in authority," "lunatics" (a very common word in his vocabulary), and others who acted according to prejudice and rules of thumb rather than according to reason carefully applied to an evolving situation—whether in making peace treaties, exchange rate decisions, unemployment policy, or mundane administrative decisions. His assessment of Beaumont Pease, chairman of Lloyds Bank, in 1924 is characteristic:

> Mr. Pease . . . deprecates thinking, or—as he prefers to call it—"the expenditure of mental agility." He desires "straightly to face the facts instead of to to find a clever way round them," and holds that, in

matters arising out of the quantity theory of money, as between brains and character, "certainly the latter does not come second in order of merit." In short, the gold standard falls within the sphere of morals or of religion, where free thought is out of place. (*JMK*, IX, 188–89)

Similarly he write to the Chancellor of the Exchequer in February 1944 concerning the Bank of England's opposition to the proposals for what would become the International Monetary Fund:

The Bank is not facing any of the realities. They do not allow for the fact that our post-war domestic policies are impossible without further American assistance. They do not allow for the fact that the Americans are strong enough to offer inducements to many or most of our friends to walk out on us, if we ostentatiously set out to start up an independent shop. They do not allow for the fact that vast debts and exiguous reserves are not, by themselves, the best qualifications for renewing old-time international banking.

Great misfortunes are not always avoided, even when there is no difficulty in foreseeing them, as we have learnt through bitter experience. I feel great anxiety that, unless a decisive decision is taken to the contrary and we move with no uncertain steps along the other path, the Bank will contrive to lead us, in new disguises, along much the same path as that which ended in 1931. That is to say, reckless gambling in the shape of assuming banking undertakings beyond what we have any means to support as soon as anything goes wrong, coupled with a policy, conceived in the interests of the old financial traditions, which pays no regard to the inescapable requirements of domestic policies. Ministers should realise that these things . . . are what the trouble is all about.

Keynes always believed that "a little clear thinking" or "more lucidity" could solve almost any problem. Throughout his career, he used every available means to achieve it, and his methods reflected his conception of the policy process and of the forces shaping public opinion. In addition, he always carried with him what Harrod calls "the presuppositions of Harvey Road"[6]— those of his youth—including the following: reform was achieved by the discussion of intelligent people; public opinion must be wisely guided; the government of Britain would be in the hands of an intellectual aristocracy using the method of persuasion.

In Keynes's view,[7] the political elite of civil servants, politicians, important journalists, and the like was open to two influences—rational persuasion and public opinion. As Keynes saw it, the elite played a dual role: not only was it privy to its own "inner opinion" but it also formed part of the "outside opinion" expressed in public speeches, newspapers, and other forms of public comment. Through its links with "outside opinion," the elite could, and in Keynes's view should, influence the public in general and prevent too large a gap emerging between the inner and outer opinions on any event. Keynes also saw the force of changing economic events as perhaps the most important other long-run determinant of opinion among the public at large. In his view, persuasion could lead to an articulation of this outside opinion, as well as alter inner opinion. Thus Keynes, in his impatience to short cut normal long-run tendencies and

[6] R. Harrod, *The Life of John Maynard Keynes*, pp. 2–5, 183, 192–93.
[7] In what follows, I draw heavily on what Keynes wrote of the process in *A Revision of the Treaty* (*JMK*, III, esp. chapter 1), discussions with Austin Robinson, and various asides elsewhere in Keynes's published and unpublished writings.

influence events in the direction he desired, saw his exercises in persuasion as performing a dual role. For they would remove and undermine old prejudices, highlight likely trends, and generally prepare the ground among the public at large, so that the elite, once persuaded, could lead rather than follow, guide rather than obfuscate. If the elite did not do so, Keynes could be rather bitter. In 1940, during his campaign for stronger wartime anti-inflationary measures, he remarked to Reginald McKenna, an old fellow campaigner:

In truth the trouble is not with public opinion at all. The public are ready for anything and as good as gold. It is the bloody politicians whose bloody minds have not been sufficiently prepared for anything unfamiliar to their ancestors. If the thing were to be sponsored and put across with responsible leadership, there would be practically no opposition at all.

Since my *Times* articles [the early version of *How to Pay for the War*] I have appreciably revised my proposals, and indeed made them a good deal more palatable to Labour. Last week I had discussions both with the Labour Front Bench and with the T.U.C. [Trades Union Congress], and enjoyed the latter particularly. What, if anything, will come of it all I do not know. Nothing, I should rather expect, until after a lag. But the public mind, judging from my fairly voluminous correspondence and discussions I have had in various groups, has made quite gigantic progress in the last two months, and in two or three months more, or at the worst six months, the fruit may be ripe on the bough.

In Keynes's view of the policy process, private meetings with ministers, M.P.s and officials, broadcasts, and articles in *The Daily Mirror* all had their part to play.

In his efforts at persuasion, particularly in the case

of the inner opinion, Keynes had great faith in rationality. He believed that individuals could rationally appreciate the appropriateness of a line of policy. Proper persuasion could wear down prejudices and inhibitions and open previously unexploited areas for choice. After all, wasn't that Keynes's experience with the 1919 peace treaties and later with the gold standard? Thus Keynes could write to T. S. Eliot in 1945 on the possibilities of a successful policy of full employment: "It may turn out I suppose, that vested interests and personal selfishness may stand in the way. But the main task is producing first the intellectual conviction and then intellectually to devise the means. Insufficiency of cleverness, not of goodness, is the main trouble. And even resistance to change as such may have many motives besides selfishness." This credo, plus his own faith in his personal powers of persuasion, provides an essential clue to many aspects of Keynes's behavior as an economist. For example, it certainly gave rise to his faith in the possibilities of active economic management, and from the 1920s often made him its most optimistic advocate. It also lay behind his approach to the 1945 American Loan negotiations—his belief that the Americans, on the basis of his masterly exposition of the case, would see (as had the British Treasury and cabinet) the sense of justice, as he called it, and offer Britain a large gift to ease the transition to peacetime conditions in the interests of the postwar world. (Characteristically, when he found his premises concerning American opinion to be untrue, he changed his ground quickly and experienced much subsequent difficulty in persuading the Treasury and the cabinet to adapt to his new appreciation of the situation.) Possibly, it also lurked behind his frequently expressed, if rather naïve, view that a rational appreciation of the situation would very often lead to a single

policy proving acceptable to opinion generally.[8] Overtones
of this point of view abound in his papers and published
work, other than his *Tract on Monetary Reform* (1923),
where he was prepared to be more catholic in his allowance for divergences in opinion. However, toward the
end of his life, Keynes at times accepted that his pre-
sumption of rationality, with its consequential effects
on his approach to the policy process, was another reflection of his early beliefs as an Apostle and member
of Bloomsbury. As he told the memoir club in 1938:

> As cause and consequence of our general state of
> mind—when young we completely misunderstood hu-
> man nature, including our own. The rationality which
> we attributed to it led to a superficiality, not only of
> judgment, but also of feeling. . . . I still suffer incur-
> ably from attributing an unreal rationality to other
> people's feeling and behaviour (and doubtless to my
> own, too). There is one small but extraordinarily silly
> manifestation of this absurd idea of what is "normal,"
> namely the impulse to *protest*—to write a letter to
> *The Times*, call a meeting in the Guildhall, subscribe
> to some fund when my presuppositions as to what is
> "normal" are not fulfilled. I behave as if there really
> existed some authority or standard to which I can
> successfully appeal if I shout loud enough—perhaps
> it is some hereditary vestige of a belief in the efficacy
> of prayer. (*JMK*, X, 448)

But Keynes did not espouse causes merely because he
was opposed to stupidity and error and wanted to in-

---

[8] Thus he could write in a February 1944 full-employment
minute, "Theoretical economic analysis has now reached a
point where it is fit to be applied. . . . [With adequate statistics]
it will all be obvious and as clear as daylight with no room
left for argument." Similarly, in *The New Statesman* of January, 28, 1939, he could imply that all the best people in
British politics were liberals like himself, who, if only they
realized it, could reduce much of the unreality of party-
political activity.

crease the scope for rationality in public affairs. He clearly had a conception of a desirable society. Unlike some of his predecessors, such as W. S. Jevons or Marshall who made some attempt to study and understand the lives of ordinary people and had decided to pursue political economy as a result of what they had learned, Keynes's conception of the desirable society was based much less on widespread observation and experience. In fact, there is no record in Keynes's case of any such observation or attempt to understand the lives of ordinary men and women beyond his strong interest in the agricultural workers on his college's estates after 1928. Although he certainly wished to improve the lives of ordinary people, Keynes's approach to the problem of doing so had its roots in the attitudes and experiences of his childhood and of Bloomsbury—in a strong but more abstractly based moral commitment to remove stupidity, waste, and absurdities. This may partially explain his greater interest in what one might call the problems of macro reform rather than those of micro reform. There is no indication that as an undergraduate or in the years immediately afterward he took any great interest in the questions of social reform that were then the subject of extensive public debate. Moreover, in the 1920s, in his attempt to change Liberal party policies, his reference to social questions centered on what he referred to as "sex questions"—"birth control and the use of contraceptives, marriage laws, the treatment of sexual offences and abnormalities, the economic position of women, the economic position of the family" (*JMK*, IX, 302–303). These perhaps had rather more to do with Bloomsbury than anything else. Finally, during World War II, his involvement with the Beveridge proposals for social insurance and allied services which set the pattern for the postwar welfare state in Britain was primarily limited to that of a good Treasury man concerned with the financial implications of the scheme and attempting to trim it down where politically easiest.[9] Nonetheless, despite its basis, Keynes's view of the good society has proved remarkably influential.

Keynes was, for want of a better word, a "neoliberal," perhaps one of the earliest. By his own admission, Keynes lay at the "liberal socialist" end of the broad spectrum of political and social thought that runs to Ludwig von Mises and Hayek and successors such as Milton Friedman at the other. From the beginning, Keynes had rejected *laissez faire* in its dogmatic form, probably more completely than had Marshall and Pigou before him. From the beginning, he emphasized the essential fragility of the economic order which others took to be natural and automatic and emphasized the need for conscious management. Thus in *Indian Currency and Finance* (1913) he noted: "The time may not be far distant when Europe, having perfected her mechanism of exchange on the basis of the gold standard, will find it possible to regulate her standard of value on a more rational and stable basis. It is not likely that we shall leave permanently the most intimate adjustments of our economic organism at the mercy of a lucky prospector, a new chemical process, or a change of ideas in Asia" (*JMK*, I, 71).

From the mid-1920s, Keynes went further and actively developed a clear "social and political philosophy." Then, in a series of essays and speeches, largely designed to shift the Liberal party from the issues that had concerned it before 1914 to ones more suited to the postwar world, he provided a statement of his political and social

---

[9] Once the scheme was trimmed, however, Keynes became its extremely powerful advocate within the Treasury. But for official opposition he would have made his maiden House of Lords speech in favor of the scheme and against ministerial inaction in 1943.

creed, which, with minor amendments, was to last him for the rest of his life.[10] Along with other essays, they clearly demonstrate that he was an extremely bad "party man," who used political parties as vehicles for his ideas and detached himself from them when they proved unhelpful. These essays also demonstrate that he regarded contemporary capitalism as a necessary, but not permanent, evil—a system which, although ugly, delivered the goods (except for a period in the 1930s) reasonably efficiently, safely channeled potentially disruptive energies into less harmful channels, and, owing to the role of convention in human affairs, capable of considerable reform without affecting its longer-term performance in accumulating the capital necessary to "solve" the economic problem. At all times, capitalism was a means, albeit a morally distasteful one, to an end, and Keynes did not believe that "there is an economic improvement for which revolution is a necessary instrument" (*JMK*, IX, 267). In the organization and management of contemporary capitalism, he saw the areas for state intervention or action, the agenda of government, as pragmatically chosen. For Keynes, the optimistic rationalist with "the presuppositions of Harvey Road," had no fear of bureaucrats and officials, provided they all held the appropriate moral outlook. As he wrote to Hayek in June 1944 on reading the latter's *Road to Serfdom:*

> I should say that what we want is not no planning, or even less planning, indeed I should say that we almost certainly want more. But the planning should take place in a community in which as many people as possible, both leaders and followers, wholly share your own liberal moral position. Moderate planning

[10] A good selection of the essays and speeches is in *JMK*, IX, part iv.

will be safe if those carrying it out are rightly orientated in their own minds and hearts to the moral issue. . . .

What we need, therefore, in my opinion, is not a change in our economic programmes, which would only lead in practice to disillusion with the results of your philosophy; but perhaps even the contrary, namely, an enlargement of them. . . . I accuse you of perhaps confusing a little bit the moral and the material issues. Dangerous acts can be done safely in a community which thinks and feels rightly, which would be the way to hell if they were executed by those who think and feel wrongly.

Keynes briefly summed up his political creed for *The New Statesman* in 1939:

The question is whether we are prepared to move out of the nineteenth century *laissez faire* state into an era of liberal socialism, by which I mean a system where we can act as an organised community for common purposes and to promote social and economic justice, whilst respecting and protecting the individual—his freedom of choice, his faith, his mind and its expression, his enterprise and his property.

It was from this position that Keynes was prepared to experiment with his, perhaps, overoptimistic view of the powers of persuasion, to release men from the yoke of drudgery and privation, to allow and encourage them to enjoy the finer things of life, both material and spiritual, and to prepare the world for "the economic possibilities for our grandchildren" when "we shall once more value ends above means and prefer the good to the useful." Thus it is not surprising that he should use a radio talk "Art and the State" to propose a massive program of public works to make the south bank of the Thames, from County Hall to Greenwich, "the equal of St. James's Park and its surroundings" or that he should take the Arts Council so seriously. Keynes always wanted to put and keep the economic problem in perspective, behind other matters of greater and more permanent significance.

Having said this, having come full circle—back to Keynes's view of the practical ends of his work as an economist—it is now time to look closely at the development of his economic ideas.

Glosses on Marshalliana, 1908–25

iii

When Keynes returned to Cambridge to teach in 1908, Alfred Marshall had just retired from the chair of political economy, and from the active teaching life of the faculty, to devote himself to writing further volumes of his *Principles of Economics*. However, his work and personality continued to dominate Cambridge economics and Keynes's economics. To understand the development of Keynes's ideas, one must first of all look briefly at the starting point, the Marshallian inheritance.

When Marshall retired, he thought that the fundamental principles of the subject were generally fixed beyond dispute. Therefore, the task of the next generation of economists would be to apply these principles to the institutions and behavior of the real world. As he put it in 1907:

Much progress has been made recently in economic science, especially on the analytical side. Disputes as to method have nearly ceased; all students accept Schmoller's dictum that analysis and the search for facts are, like the right and left foot in walking, each nearly useless alone; but that the two are strong in combination.

Again, what by the chemical analogy may be called *qualitative* analysis has done the greater part of its work—that is to say, there is a general agreement as to the characters and directions of the changes which various economic forces tend to produce. . . .

Much less progress has indeed been made towards the *quantitative* determination of the relative strength of different economic forces. . . .[1]

Marshall's legacy to his successors was a system of analysis. Although in the appendices to the *Principles* and in Marshall's earlier work there are important contributions to the general equilibrium model of economists with its conception of the general interdependence of all elements in the economic system, his construction of the apparatus of partial equilibrium analysis, the set of tools to analyze phenomena in small sectors of the economy—firms, industries—using the assumption of *ceteris paribus*,[2] turned attention toward the determinants of supply and demand—prices, costs, tastes, and so forth. Although this apparatus was essentially static, and designed for analyzing equilibrium situations, it did, in skillful hands such as Marshall's allow for the consideration of changes occurring through time. This

[1] A. C. Pigou, ed., *Memorials of Alfred Marshall* (London, 1925), pp. 323–24.
[2] "All other things remaining equal" on the assumption that the repercussions of changes in the area under consideration are so small relative to the aggregate of economic activity that they can safely be ignored.

partial analysis, with its emphasis on one thing at a time and on supply and demand, was an important influence on Keynes's method.

As Keynes's place in the Marshallian program of research was in the monetary field, one must look at the development of Marshall's thought in this area as a background to Keynes's own contributions.

When Keynes began to work in this field, Marshallian monetary theory existed more as a Cambridge oral tradition than as a matter of textbook economics—a sharp contrast to the theory of value, which had appeared in the *Principles*. For although money was one of Marshall's favorite topics for lectures, beyond what came out in evidence before Royal Commissions in the 1880s and 1890s and odd articles with occasional references to the trade cycle, he made no systematic attempt to present his ideas until, in his declining years, he prepared *Money Credit and Commerce* (1923).[3] For our purposes, we need to consider three strands of Marshall's teaching: his development of the cash balances approach to the quantity equation which purports to show the determinants of the value of money, his theory of the rate of interest, and his theory of business fluctuations.

The cash balances approach. Within the classical tradition, there have been two broad ways of looking at the determinants of the value of money in an economy. The first has been associated with the name of Irving Fisher.

---

[3] In his treatment of value theory, Marshall had assumed that the value of money was constant. One of the effects of Marshall's virtual neglect of monetary theory in his published work was that money tended to live in a separate economic box from the rest of economics—a fate it enjoyed elsewhere, however, and has enjoyed again to a considerable extent since the academic digestion of the Keynesian revolution, originally designed in part to end the split (see below, pp. 161–64).

It simply linked the price level (P) with the quantity of money in circulation (M), its velocity or efficiency (V), and the physical volume of trade (T), and took the form $MV \equiv PT$. The second, associated with Marshall, but most fully developed by his successors, in particular Keynes and A. C. Pigou, had a long tradition in English economics going back to William Petty and John Locke. It arose in Marshall's case from attempting to apply to money the general supply-and-demand analysis used elsewhere in his work. In Marshall's formulation, the demand for cash balances (m)[4] depended on the proportion of real income (or wealth) the community wished to hold in the form of cash (k), the price level (p), and the level of real income (or wealth) (Y).[5] It therefore took the form $m \equiv kpY$. In discussions of the long run, Marshall tended to adopt the Fisherine approach, emphasizing changes in V and T. However, in short-period discussions, he tended to work with the cash balances approach with its elasticity and ability to deal easily with changes in such things as expectations and confidence, which might effect k.[6] Marshall also spent some time, as did Fisher, worrying about the appropriate use of index numbers to represent the purchasing power of

[4] I use different symbols to make clear that the two approaches might, and do, require differing definitions of the magnitudes under consideration.
[5] In Marshall's writings, income and wealth tend to be used interchangeably in discussing the demand for money. Of course, in long-run equilibrium the two concepts would bear a determinate relationship to one another. In the same circumstances the two versions of the quantity equation would also be equivalent, as every variable would have determinate relation to every other.
[6] In Marshall's models, the cash balances approach was never presented with a banking system. However, bank lending appeared through the effects of changes in bank reserves (resulting from changes in the supply of gold or convertible paper currency) on discount rates and the volume of loans.

money. Of Marshall's pupils, only Keynes was to have the same interest.

The theory of the rate of interest. Marshall clearly distinguished between the real and the money rates of interest. The former was determined by the supply and demand for real investible resources, while the latter was determined by the supply and demand for loans in the market.[7] According to Marshall, the source of supply of capital was savings, the volume of which would vary *over the long run* with the level of income and would also be to some extent directly responsive to the rate of interest—although security as to social and political conditions in the future, the willingness to wait for future enjoyment of wealth and family affection could also be important in determining secular changes. This real rate of interest ruled the roost and drew the money rate toward it, that rate being the result of the supply and demand for loans, after divergences of relatively short duration. Throughout his analysis, the real rate of interest was independent of the supply of money, being the product of the underlying forces of productivity and thrift in the economy. However, the price of loans could in the short period be affected by changes in the supply of money.

The Theory of the trade cycle. In the long run, in Marshall, money was merely a flux of easing transaction: it was neutral in that it had no effect of the equilibrium values of the real variables. In addition, its absolute quantity did not affect its role as a flux. Moreover, in the short period, since Marshall excluded bank deposits from the definition of money, changes in its quantity

[7] The reader should note that Marshall's use of the term real rate of interest differs from contemporary usage. The contemporary usage, derived from Fisher, defines the real rate as the money (or nominal) rate adjusted for the *expected* rate of inflation during the term of the loan.

normally had more to do with short-period balance-of-payments movements than anything else, and here Marshall (assuming by analogy from the individual firm that competition always led to full utilization of capacity and concentrating on the balance of trade rather than the full set of components of the balance of payments)[8] tended to assume that their duration would be short-lived and their magnitude small. Thus he concentrated on changes in real variables, expectations, and credit variables, when he turned to discussions of the trade cycle itself.

As J. S. Mill had before him, Marshall, while recognizing that deficient aggregate demand could exist in exceptional periods following episodes of widespread speculation culminating in a financial crisis, generally assumed in his analysis that capital and labor were fully employed. He had a theory of the credit cycle, during phases of which there might be short-term unemployment; but he did not have a developed theory of a production, employment, or trade cycle depending on fluctuations in the level of aggregate demand.

Marshall's credit cycle had its origins in changes in real variables—harvests, wars or threats of wars, inventions. Such changes led to changes in businessmen's expectations, errors of optimism and pessimism as he called them, which the banking system magnified. Thus an event that brought about a favorable shift in expectations led businessmen, financed by the credit system which now took a more favorable view of paper promises to pay, to increase their demand for inputs of goods and labor. This pushed up wages, prices, and profits. Many speculators, experiencing the rise in prices and thinking it would continue, bought goods with the expectation of

---

[8] The balance of payments includes trade flows, invisible items, investment items, and reserve movements.

selling them at a profit, thus giving a further twist to the upward movement. The expansion continued, with more and more activity taking place with credit and borrowed money, until lenders began to read the signs of the times and began to contract their loans, which affected both speculators and businessmen undertaking longer-term capital projects. Speculators sold some of their goods to pay their debts and by so doing brought a check to the rise in prices. At this point, distrust replaced confidence, and the change in expectations led to a "commercial storm" as businessmen tried to adjust their positions. There followed a "dull heavy calm" in which businessmen were unwilling to undertake new ventures before confidence returned.

Marshall laid some emphasis on the effects of rigidities in the system, particularly those in wages, salaries, and other business charges. Thus the failure of wages and salaries to vary fully with prices over the cycle had the effect of aggravating it, as profits increased even further in the upswing and fell even further in the downswing. Similarly, changes in the public's holdings of money balances over the cycle aggravated it further, with shifts into goods increasing prices during the upswing and shifts into money balances doing the reverse during the downswing.

As for remedies for the cycle and the discontinuities in employment it caused, Marshall accepted that it was impossible to remedy harvest fluctuations and undesirable to reduce the flow of inventions. He turned to consider ways of increasing businessmen's knowledge of the underlying situation, so as to reduce the errors of optimism and pessimism—including more work in economic science and a body of disinterested men to forecast "trade storms and trade weather generally," and changes in the monetary and banking system that would serve to prevent such errors as remained from having such severe effects. These monetary changes included the establishment of a stable standard of value, the raising of the normal cash reserve of the system to reduce the importance of credit, and the use of the discount rate of the central bank to check unreasonable expansions of credit. However, he was opposed to, or supported very weakly, various schemes involving governmental intervention, largely on the long-term grounds that they would hinder the freedom on which long-term progress depended and bring money into politics with disastrous results.

Prior to the 1920s Keynes's contributions to economics were noted less for their theoretical innovations than for their realistic acumen and their very good understanding of the working of complex institutions. This is shown in his discussions of the Indian currency system and of the economic problems created by World War I.

Although it seems very odd now, the subject of currency arrangements for India was, before 1914, one of the most discussed subjects in British monetary economics. After 1873 an increasing number of countries at the center of the international monetary system, formally or informally, abandoned bimetallism, under which gold and silver were convertible at a fixed ratio, and adopted a gold-standard regime. The resulting decline in the demand for silver for official reserves, plus the expansion in the supply of silver owing to new discoveries, produced a decline in the world market price of silver, and this had important effects on the exchange rates of those countries whose currencies remained on a silver standard (one unit of domestic currency being equal to a given quantity of silver). India remained on a silver standard until 1893, when, after the breakdown of negotiations for the restoration of bimetallism, she closed her mints to the free coinage of silver, because the depreciation of the gold value of silver inconvenienced trade and disturbed public finance. Following this, the Fowler Commission recommended in 1899 that India should take steps to institute a gold standard of the orthodox British type with internal circulation of gold coin. However, events did not work out like that, and a different system evolved in response to the particular situations which arose as the result of *ad hoc* measures on the part of the authorities responsible. This regime came under severe strain during 1907–08 and discussion naturally ensued as to what to do about the system.

Keynes, with his India Office experience, turned to the question in six lectures at the London School of Economics in 1910 (which he later gave in Cambridge early in 1911), in a paper to the Royal Economic Society meeting in May 1911, and in *Indian Currency and Finance*, before his appointment to the Royal Commission set up to investigate the problem in 1913. He took the view that the system that had evolved, a gold exchange standard whereby India kept her exchange rate pegged to sterling not through gold flows but through official purchases and sales of a gold convertible currency (in this particular case, sterling), put India "in the forefront of monetary progress" (*JMK*, I, 182). He suggested that this system, which economized on gold, was "the ideal currency of the future" (*JMK*, I, 25). His book is notable for its exposition of the detailed working of such a system and for its suggestions for improving the organization of the Indian banking system, most particularly for the establishment of a central bank, a project for which he naturally provided the appropriate blueprint and advocacy, and which occupied much of his energy as a member of the Royal Commission. In this advocacy he was successful to a large extent, although the ensuing war meant that the commission's report was not acted upon.

The book, along with the related discussion, is also notable for its firm pre-1914 air of Marshallian certainty. For all his discussion of innovations in monetary practice, Keynes accepted a gold standard world of unchangeable exchange rates in which the strains of such small and short-lived international disequilibria that did occur could be taken care of by short-term international capital flows properly influenced by changes in central bank discount rates. Throughout, as one commentator has said, "it was, under the long shadow of Ricardo, supposed that invisible hands would smooth . . . [disequilibria] out, under the cover of slightly discordant trade cycles."[9] This meant that his analysis of short-term central bank policy was largely limited to conditions of short-term financial or speculative crisis, where the traditional rule of English central banking (established by the time of and under the influence of Walter Bagehot)—unlimited accommodation at a price —was all that was necessary. Only the difficulties of World War I and its aftermath were gradually to change such presumptions on the part of Keynes and his contemporaries, whether practitioners or theorists.

When war came in 1914, Keynes was immediately caught up in the government's handling of financial turmoil that enveloped the City. He then returned to Cambridge for a term, during which he lectured on the economic problems of the war. His first lecture opened with a remark that signaled the beginning of a shift away from the relatively long-term orientation of most of Marshall's work toward Keynes's short-period concerns: "The War upsets many of the maxims of the economists, who take long views and preach against snatching small, temporary gains. Now it is sometimes worthwhile to snatch such benefits and to do things which it would be very foolish to do permanently."

In January 1915 he returned to Whitehall and within months he became a part of the regular Treasury staff dealing with the financial side of the war.[10] During the next four and a half years his output of reports and memoranda was substantial and covered a wide range of problems. Personally he moved in the highest circles, both in the office and outside, especially on weekends: his letters to his parents are full of reports of dinners with Lloyd George, weekends with Lord Cunliffe (the governor of the Bank of England), the Asquiths, and the McKennas, to name only a few. From this period his papers of greatest interest are those on the broadest questions of war finance: especially internal borrowing, inter-Allied finance, the raising of dollars for expenditure in America, and exchange-rate support, and, toward the end of the war, reparations problems. Like his Indian contributions, they show a firm grasp of intricate detail and of economic interrelationships. Thus, once 1915 had passed, Keynes began to approach every problem as a problem of a full-employment economy in which the authorities could expect little more from restricting consumption, by taxation, or further inducements to save, and in which any addition to expenditure, for British forces or supplies for her Allies, or any reduction of factor supplies (through, for example, conscription) would, through a reduction of exports or an increase in imports, spill over in the balance of payments (or, in the circumstances operating during most of the war, the need to make dollar payments in New York). These same circumstances, plus the fact that

[10] Early in 1917 the Finance Division was broken up and Keynes made head of the part concerned with overseas finance, one of his major concerns before then.

the support for a cheap pound in the form of short-term capital movements would be unavailable, enabled Keynes to argue successfully on several occasions against proposals to remove the peg supporting the sterling exchange so as to increase the real resources available to Britain for the prosecution of the war. Throughout, his analysis was basically Marshallian, even though the situations were hardly foreseen by Marshall.

In the closing stages of the war and the first months of the peace after the armistice, Keynes's concern with inter-Allied finance brought him more and more into contact with Americans. To them, he often appeared "rude, dogmatic and disobliging" (*JMK*, XVI, 264),[11] sentiments that were to appear again in World War II. As in that later war, however, he soon developed very good working relationships with many of his American counterparts. He also began to learn of the trials and tribulations of negotiating with Americans: the lack of executive control over Congress, the sensitiveness of American officials to public criticism, the dangers of assuming that the understanding of expert financial negotiators is reflected across a continent. And, as he was to sum it up in the middle of the experience of the later war:

> Remember that, in a negotiation lasting weeks, the situation is entirely fluid up to almost the last moment. Everything you are told, even with the greatest appearance of authority and decision, is provisional, without commitment, "thinking out loud," a kite, a trial balloon. There is no orderly progression towards the final conclusion. Thus you must not believe that a man is not your loyal friend, merely because he has raised false hopes, or run out on you, or even, from a strict point of view, double-crossed you. Equally, do not become faint-hearted against opposition. You may

[11] The words are those of Basil Blackett, a Treasury colleague.

be able, when things look worst, to gain a sudden reversal in your favour. All this is a process, unfamiliar to us, of discovering by open trial and error what will go and what will not. I liken them to bees who for weeks will fly round in all directions with no ascertainable destination, providing both the menace of stings and the hope of honey; and, at last, perhaps because the queen in the White Hive has emitted some faint, indistinguishable odour, suddenly swarm to a single spot in a compact, impenetrable bunch.[12]

His other major preoccupation was the preparation for and the negotiating of the peace treaties. The preparations largely concerned the exploration, from various points of view, of the reparations prospect. However, as the senior Treasury official on the British delegation to the Paris Peace Conference and the official representative of the British Empire on the Supreme Economic Council, Keynes was also concerned with much wider issues, such as relief, German food supplies, inter-Allied debts, and financial reconstruction, as well as the peace treaties themselves. Disillusioned and disheartened by the terms of the treaties, he resigned from the Treasury and left the conference in June 1919 to regain the freedom of private life.

With the encouragement of Jan Smuts, who had also hesitated over the treaties but stayed and signed them, and of others, Keynes at white heat turned to the writing of *The Economic Consequences of the Peace*, which appeared in British bookshops in December 1919.[13] As

[12] "The Washington Negotiations for Lend Lease in Stage II," December 12, 1944.
[13] Keynes wrote three other pieces as a result of his experiences at the peace conference, "Lloyd George: A Fragment," originally a part of *Economic Consequences* but removed before publication, which first appeared in 1933; "Melchior: A Defeated Enemy," a memoir read to the Bloomsbury memoir

the economist Joseph Schumpeter put it in the obituary notice he wrote on Keynes, the book "met with a reception that makes the word *success* sound commonplace and insipid."[14] It ranks as one of the finest pamphlets written in the field of political economy and is, perhaps, a classic in the English language, both for its contents and for its influence on affairs. Although in many respects—in its subject matter and modes of analysis— the book falls outside the works essential to a discussion of Keynes's development as an economist, its importance and the controversy it raised, including the charge during World War II that it was to some extent responsible for appeasement and the rise of Hitler, require us to look more closely at it.

In some respects *Economic Consequences* is three books in one: a trenchant political pamphlet attacking the morality of the peace treaties in the light of the understandings at the time of the armistice, a technical discussion of the economic provisions of the treaties, and an interesting discussion and critique of the economic relationships among nations and classes before 1914. The three books are closely interwoven and enlivened by vivid, mordant, and arresting portraits of the major personalities involved at Paris and Versailles: Wilson, Lloyd George, and Clemenceau. Thus of Clemenceau he wrote:

> He felt of France what Pericles felt of Athens— unique value in her, nothing else mattering; but his theory of politics was Bismarck's. He had one illusion

club in 1931–32, which appeared in 1949; and "A meeting of the Council of Three," a working up of rough notes from such a meeting (a copy of which went to Sir Maurice Hankey) in the course of a reading party with friends in 1925, and which remained unpublished until 1972. (All three pieces appear in *JMK*, X.)

[14] *American Economic Review*, September 1946.

—France; and one disillusion—mankind, including Frenchmen, and his colleagues not least. . . . Prudence required some measure of lip service to the "ideals" of foolish Americans and hypocritical Englishmen; but it would be stupid to believe that there is much room in the world, as it really is, for such affairs as the League of Nations, or any sense in the principle of self-determination except as an ingenious formula for rearranging the balance of power in one's own interests. (*JMK*, II, 20)

Leaving aside the moral issue, Keynes's message in *Economic Consequences* was that "the Carthaginian peace is not *practically* right or possible. . . . You cannot restore Central Europe to 1870 without setting up such strains in the European structure and letting loose human and spiritual forces as . . . will overwhelm not only you and your 'guarantees,' but your institutions, and the existing order of your society" (*JMK*, II, 23).

To argue this point, he started with a typically Keynesian premise: that the supposedly automatic and natural economic progress that Europe had experienced before the war had rested on four unstable and peculiar bases. The first had been the system of international interdependence that had allowed the population of central Europe, especially Germany, to expand and produce industrial exports to pay for imports of food and raw materials. The second had been the minimal role that tariffs, differing currency systems, and frontiers played in the economic life of central Europe on which the economies of the rest of the Continent were heavily dependent. The third had been the psychology of prewar European society, which had so arranged its affairs to favor the maximum accumulation of capital—the psychology of accepted inequality tempered by the stable understanding that those who received the bulk of the rewards deferred consumption in favor of saving. The final element in the system had been the favorable terms on which Europe had been able to exchange manufactured goods for food from the areas of new settlement. All of these, he argued, had been shattered in varying degrees by the war, and, therefore, their restoration, and European rehabilitation, should have been the first task of those responsible for the peace.

Keynes then went on to examine the treaties themselves and argue that the sums the Allies expected to gain from Germany (and her allies) in indemnities were excessive and impossible to obtain; that the impossibility of their obtaining them was due in part to the cumulative effects of the other parts of the treaties on the economic life of central Europe; and that in the light of his assumptions, or vision, concerning the nature of the European economic system before the war the other parts of the treaties were themselves unwise and suicidal. On several occasions, the discussion shows signs of haste and the desire to make a good case seem even stronger by relegating important qualifications to the footnotes. Nevertheless, the case seemed convincing to his contemporaries, particularly in England, and the book, along with Keynes's later writings, had an important effect in the change in opinion which made a later scaling down of reparations possible, *after* Germany had suffered considerable social and economic damage. The book also had its effects on Anglo-French relations, as the British, desiring to be rid of much of the treaties, paid insufficient attention to the French desires for the feeling, if not the reality, of security against future German aggression. Finally, although it did not affect in any important respect, the American decision not to ratify the treaties, it helped to form the attitudes that favored American isolationism in the interwar years.

So much for its political effects. What of its economics? Here one must approach Keynes's work at several levels. First, as regards his vision of Europe before 1914, it is clear that he was only partially right. Certainly frontiers were important—as the economic disintegration of the European economy during the interwar years was to indicate. Certainly, as well, the psychological conditions surrounding the nineteenth-century process of accumulation were fragile, a fact that is only too clear to this generation, with its repeated social conflict over the distribution of the cake most frequently manifest in the process of wage inflation. However, Keynes underestimated the resilience of economies, their ability to recover from the brink (or even the pit) of disaster, as the experience of Germany after 1923 and the European and Japanese economies after 1945 clearly indicate. Moreover, Keynes's worries about the reappearance of the Malthusian devil and the tendency for the terms of trade between primary products and manufactured goods to turn automatically against the latter to the detriment of European standards of life (the latter reflecting long-standing Cambridge assumptions that lasted beyond World War II) seem, in the light of the events he was discussing, misplaced—and may still be so today, despite a recurrence of neo-Malthusianism among certain economists and others.

As for the second problem—the actual terms of the peace applied particularly to Germany in 1919, and their feasibility—the debate continues. The demand for reparations, part in kind and part in cash over a period of years, first was scaled down and then broke down in the interwar period, although the sums involved in the Young Settlement of 1929 continue to be paid by post-1945 West Germany. Apart from the deliveries in kind and, to a lesser extent, the cash payments, which played an important role in the fate of the German economy up to 1923 with its spectacular hyperinflation, reparations payments were balanced by foreign borrowing until

1928–29. After that, they were effectively transferred in terms of a current account surplus until the summer of 1931, but at costs to the German economy (and subsequently to the rest of the world) that many regard as unacceptable. True, after 1870 France had effected the transfer of a relatively larger indemnity, initially at least through foreign borrowing, and the "market" effected almost as large a transfer in the form of British overseas investment before 1914, but neither of these cases, achieved in particular historical circumstances, settles the case for the demands made on Germany in 1919. And so the debate continues.

Keynes continued to contribute to the discussion of the German reparations problem after 1919, in the form of another book (*A Revision of the Treaty*, 1922) and a mass of newspaper and professional journal articles (*JMK*, XVII, XVIII, IX), not to mention his contributions to the British (and to a minor extent, American) discussions of the post-1945 treatment of Germany. However, the point has come to turn back toward his main area of interest, monetary theory, and policy.

Keynes's resignation from the Treasury in 1919 and the success of the *Economic Consequences* marked another change in his career and way of life. For he did not return to his heavy prewar load of teaching and supervision in Cambridge. Although he normally continued to give one set of eight lectures each year, to supervise selected pupils, and to take an active part in the life of his college, especially as bursar, he resigned the Girdlers' Lectureship in Economics that he held since 1911, and turned to a secondary career in the City and journalism. This change of direction affected the form his work as an economist took, but not its content.

Between the end of the war and the mid-1920s Keynes's contributions to the discussion of monetary issues centered primarily around the problems faced by the British economy; the appropriate exchange-rate policy after the cessation of hostilities; the use of monetary policy during the postwar boom and slump; and the most appropriate monetary regime for the country once matters had more or less returned to normal. On each problem (other than the first, which arose while he was still a member of the Treasury), Keynes found himself consulted by the authorities responsible for the decisions.[15] He also attempted to use more public means of persuasion in favor of the line of policy he thought desirable in the circumstances. We thus have a good record of the evolution of his views during these years.

Keynes's advice on exchange-rate policy, given in January 1919, after the cessation of hostilities, provided one of the only "plans" for dealing with this aspect of the transition from war to peace. From January 1916 onward, using the proceeds of security sales and new borrowing in New York to supplement current earnings of foreign exchange, the authorities had pegged the pound sterling at just over $4.76. At the end of the war, which had badly disrupted the cost, price, and other economic relationships underlying prewar exchange rates, the authorities found themselves in need of an exchange rate policy. Treasury and Bank of England opinion, as well as the Cunliffe Committee appointed to consider the matter, accepted a return to the gold standard at the prewar parity of $4.86 as the ultimate goal of policy, but as those concerned expected the restoration of the prewar order to take up to ten years, there was

[15] The first instance of consultation took place within two months of the publication of *The Economic Consequences of the Peace*, a fact which calls into question his official biographer's suggestion that after the publication of the book "he remained an outlaw from British official circles for many years afterwards" (R. Harrod, *The Life of John Maynard Keynes*, p. 254).

considerable room for disagreement as to the best short-term policy. Into the resulting situation, where the recommendations ranged from immediate postwar deflation to restore sterling to prewar par to "wait and see," perhaps with a floating exchange rate, Keynes produced a plan that accepted some depreciation of sterling from prewar par through a scheme whose centerpiece was a variable tax on exports of gold. Unlike many of his colleagues, he did not favor a deliberate postwar deflation to reduce British prices sufficiently to appreciate the exchange rate to par. He preferred to aim at price stability by accepting the 10-15–per-cent depreciation of the exchange rate which he thought had occurred, and preventing further domestic or international inflation by allowing only tax reductions by administrative order, thus effectively restoring the prewar gold-standard mechanism at the depreciated exchange rate. The plan fell by the wayside in the months of policy confusion that followed, and the authorities met the situation by allowing sterling to float in March 1919.

When the postwar inflation came, as it did in a boom that lasted for just over a year after April 1919, Keynes made several contributions to contemporary discussions of monetary policy. At that time, the Treasury rather than the Bank of England had effective control of interest-rate policy through its policy of borrowing at short term from the market through Treasury bills available in unlimited quantities at a time when the central government current account was (at least initially) in deficit and the short-term debt requiring continual refinancing was very large. In these circumstances, if the Bank of England attempted to change its lending rate—to which a large number of interest rates in the financial sector were linked—without a parallel movement of Treasury bill rates, sales of Treasury bills to the public would fall off and the Bank, as banker to the government, would be obliged to provide the necessary accommodation, thus undoing the tightening of monetary conditions implicit in the rise in its lending rate (or Bank rate). During October and November of 1919 the authorities brought the relatively cheap money of the wartime and early postwar periods to an end with the raising of the Treasury bill rate from 3.5 to 5 per cent (Bank rate went from 5 to 6 per cent). Soon afterward, the government publicly accepted the recommendations of the Cunliffe Committee (which the Treasury had already privately used as the basis of its policy for some months) for limiting the fiduciary issue (backed by the issue of government securities rather than gold) of wartime Currency Notes. On the then existing monetary arrangements, this meant that any increased demand for currency—either for transactions purposes or for bank reserves—that would result from the continuing inflation would bring on a fall in the Bank of England's free gold reserves and, given the conventions of the day, a further rise in interest rates. When the pressure for a further rise in rates came in due course, among those consulted by Austen Chamberlain, the Chancellor, was Keynes, who had earlier supported the limitation of the fiduciary issue and its logical consequence, "a very high bank Rate."[16]

When consulted by the Chancellor in an interview on February 4, 1920, which he supplemented by a long note sent in afterward, Keynes argued that a moderate increase in rates might have little effect beyond making government borrowing more expensive. Therefore a stiff dose of very dear money was essential to check infla-

[16] During the boom period of nine months prior to January 1920, the cost of living had risen by 12.5 per cent and wholesale prices by 36 per cent. The ultimate rises in that cycle were 35 and 51 per cent respectively.

tion. In the Chancellor's words, written after the interview: "K would go for a financial crisis (doesn't believe it would lead to unemployment). Would go to whatever rate is necessary—perhaps 10% —and keep it at that for three years." From Keynes's supporting memorandum, plus the rough notes he made for a lecture on "The Future of Interest," it is possible to see his position at the time more clearly. He argued that, without the reimposition of wartime controls on borrowing and materials' allocations, the only way to break the inflationary boom was to reduce the demand for current savings (themselves insensitive to changes in the rate of interest in the short period).[17] A sharp dose of dear money would change businessmen's expectations of future prices and profits and hence reduce their current demand for savings to finance inventories and investment. This, he argued, would not cause any serious unemployment, as there was a wide margin of safety before industry found itself working below full capacity, given that much of the current problem was speculative. However, unlike many of the Chancellor's other advisers, Keynes did not advocate dear money in order to get back to the gold standard. Rather, his advocacy rested on the damage inflation would do to the structure of contemporary society—a theme he had touched on in *The Economic Consequences of the Peace* (*JMK*, II, 149*ff*) and was to return to later. Also, unlike most of the Chancellor's other advisers except R. G. Hawtrey, Keynes laid great stress on the effects of changes in monetary policy on businessmen's expectations, although he allowed that such changes might take some time to become effective.

[17] Keynes believed, as Marshall had before him, that the volume of savings was relatively very insensitive to changes in the rate of interest—a view he continued to hold throughout his working life as an economist.

It is probably wise at this point to note that the events of 1920 represented one of the few occasions of policy advice that Keynes looked back on from the perspective of his own later ideas. He did this almost twenty-two years later, when he arranged for the collection and preservation of the official papers relating to the episode. His note on the papers ran as follows:

These papers which Mr. Waley has dug out are fascinating and call back one's mind to a vanished age. As usual the economists were found to be unanimous and the common charge to the contrary without foundation!

What impresses me most is the complete hopelessness of the situation. All controls had been abandoned. It was not politically possible to reintroduce rationing. There was no capital control. The notion of disciplining the joint stock banks, who seem to have been extraordinarily truculent and independent, was outside the philosophy of the age. . . . With all the methods of control, then so unorthodox, excluded, I feel myself that I should give today exactly the same advice that I gave them, namely a swift and severe dose of dear money, sufficient to break the market, and quick enough to prevent at least some of the disastrous consequences that would otherwise ensue. In fact the remedies of the economists were taken, but too timidly. I should doubt today whether even if they had been taken drastically by any means all of the evils of 1921 could have been avoided.

I propose to write a separate paper on the lessons of this for the next time. . . .

If the vast bulk of purchasing power, which must necessarily exist at the end of the war, is released in psychological conditions surrounding the end of the war, the result cannot be different from what it was in 1919 to 1921.

Simultaneously with the authorities' decision to raise Bank rate to 7 per cent on April 15, 1920, the inflationary boom broke and Britain experienced one of the sharpest slumps in her history, with wholesale prices and the cost of living falling from their 1920 peaks by more than 50 and 35 per cent respectively. Although in 1921, as in 1920, Keynes was primarily preoccupied with the results of the 1919 peace treaties and the efforts to implement or alter them, in the third of a series of five articles in *The Sunday Times* during August and September 1921, at the bottom of the slump, he attempted to explain the origins of the slump and outline the appropriate policy. To put it briefly, the explanation was very Marshallian, as had been the analysis underlying the policy advice of 1920. Keynes explained fluctuations in terms of the by then conventional model of businessmen's errors of optimism and pessimism in a growing economy—the errors themselves representing businessmen's reactions to changing real and, to a subsidiary extent, monetary phenomena. To reduce the scope of such errors, Keynes saw that monetary policy, directed at the cost of short-term credit through changes in Bank rate, could influence businessmen's price (and profit) expectations and, therefore, their behavior through the effects of the changing interest rates on traders' decisions to hold stocks.

Keynes's theory of monetary policy at this time was similar to that consistently held by R. G. Hawtrey in a series of books and articles that stretch from 1913 to his recent death.[18] Though Keynes came, in the course of the next few years, to have serious doubts about the interest-sensitivity of traders' decisions to hold stocks,

---

[18] Before 1914 Hawtrey had been the only "monetarist" member of what has been called the Cambridge School, the others relatively playing down the role of money in the economy.

as he would explain at length in *A Treatise on Money* (1930) and as he discussed at great length with Hawtrey then and afterward, he continued to share Hawtrey's interventionist approach to monetary policy and his emphasis on expectations. Thus he could write to Hawtrey in 1930, "I feel that ultimately I am joined in common agreement with you as against most of the rest of the world," and in 1937 call him "my grandparent . . . in the paths of errancy" (*JMK*, XIII, 132; XIV, 202*n*).

The lines of thought nascent in the 1920 advice and the 1921 article became much clearer in Keynes's *A Tract on Monetary Reform* (1923), itself largely a reworking of newspaper articles published in 1922. There, the framework of analysis was firmly Marshallian, although the actual exposition naturally reflected the development of Marshall's analysis by other members of the Cambridge School. For example, his exposition of the cash balances approach to the determination of the value of money followed on from both Marshall and Pigou in taking the form $n \equiv p(k + rk')$, where n represented the currency notes and other forms of cash in circulation with the public, p the price of a consumption unit (i.e., the cost of living), k and k' the equivalent number of consumption units kept by the public in currency and bank deposits respectively, and r the cash reserves kept by the banks against their deposit liabilities. As with Marshall's formulation, the amount of k and k' depended on both habits and the wealth (or income) of the community in question. The thrust of the analysis, however, was much more toward short-term problems than had been the case previously, for, as Keynes put it after outlining the version of the cash balances approach set out above: "But the *long run* is a misleading guide to current affairs. *In the long run* we are all dead. Economists set themselves too easy, too useless a task if in tempestuous seasons they can only tell us that when the storm is long past the ocean is flat again" (*JMK*, IV, 65).[19]

Much of the *Tract* was devoted to an outline of the effects of changes in the price level on various groups in society and on the level of business activity. As a result of this analysis, Keynes came down as follows:

> Thus inflation is unjust and deflation is inexpedient. Of the two perhaps deflation is, if we rule out exaggerated inflations such as that of Germany, the worse; because it is worse, in an impoverished world, to provoke unemployment than to disappoint the *rentier*. But it is not necessary to weigh one evil against the other. It is easier to agree that both are evils to be shunned. The individualistic capitalism of today, precisely because it entrusts saving to the individual investor and production to the individual employer, presumes a stable measuring rod of value, and cannot be efficient—perhaps cannot survive—without one. (*JMK*, IV, 36)

In fact, the *Tract* represented a sustained argument in favor of the authorities' active management of the monetary system to preserve price stability and contained a series of suggestions as to the means of achieving this end. Throughout, nothing appeared in the theoretical passages that did not help to further Keynes's purposes. For example, the discussion of the theory of exchange-rate determination and the operation of futures (or forward) markets in foreign exchange was directly related to Keynes's proposal that, in the circumstances, official national policies to preserve price sta-

---

[19] Despite this statement, the assumptions of the fundamental formal analysis were strictly those of the long run. For example, his shifts between income and wealth in discussing the determinants of k assume long-run equilibrium, as noted above (p. 45, *n* 5). Similarly, throughout the *Tract* Keynes assumed that unemployment was a short-term aberration in the system, as had Marshall.

bility through the operation of monetary policy required a regime of flexible (or more strictly interpreted, adjustable) exchange rates to insulate the economy from inflationary or deflationary movements developing abroad. Similarly, the discussion of Cambridge monetary theory related directly to a discussion of how, using Bank rate policy and open-market purchases and sales of government securities, the authorities could so manage businessmen's expectations of future price levels, or their costs of production and investment within a given set of price expectations, as to result in their behaving in a manner that would preserve price stability. In this discussion, however, traders' stock played a less important role than they had in the 1921 article discussed above.

The *Tract* represented a distinct break from the Cambridge tradition of Marshall, Pigou, and most of their pupils in its activism and its emphasis on position management rather than changes in such things as the rules regarding bank behavior. This theme of active monetary management now received even more attention from Keynes, initially in the discussions surrounding Britain's return to the gold standard in 1925.

As noted above, after the end of World War I Britain allowed her exchange rates with other currencies to depend on market variations in supply and demand. However, soon after the war the accepted aim of official policy became a return to a fixed exchange-rate system and sterling pegged to gold (hence to other currencies) on prewar terms. In the *Tract*, as earlier in articles in *The Manchester Guardian*, Keynes had raised several questions concerning official policy. The first, he phrased as "devaluation versus deflation": should the exchange rate be fixed near its existing market value, which was below the prewar value, or should the exchange rate be raised through domestic deflation to the prewar value? The second, he phrased as "stability of prices versus stability of exchange": should Britain attempt to keep her domestic price level stable or stabilize the exchange rate and adjust domestic prices to it? Although he allowed that others might plausibly hold opinions that differed from his, in the years 1923–25 Keynes campaigned against an attempt to return to the gold standard through domestic deflation in the press, in public speeches, and, as the authorities moved to take the fatal decision, in evidence to the secret Treasury Committee set up to consider the issue and in private consultations with the Chancellor just before the government made the decision. Initially he campaigned on the grounds that his proposed regime of domestic price stability with flexible exchange rates was preferable to a return to the gold standard. As matters came to a head, he turned increasingly to the argument that the exchange rate which the authorities were aiming at was too high, given the international competitive position of the British economy, and that an attempt to adopt it would—through the resulting decline in exports and rise in imports and the high interest rates that would be necessary to attract short-term capital to London to prevent losses of official gold reserves—lead to deflation in Britain. This deflationary pressure would continue until British relative prices and costs adjusted to the new situation—implying, in the absense of inflation abroad, a fall in British wage rates, along with the social strife this entailed.

Despite the fact that those responsible for the final decision treated Keynes as a serious critic of a policy of returning to gold, the official documents now available show that they never really met his argument squarely during the decision-taking process. They resorted instead to strategic assumptions that removed Keynes's problems, or argued, using traditional theory, that in the long run everything would be satisfactory without really specifying how long the long run would be. The upshot was that on April 28, 1925, Chancellor of the Exchequer Winston Churchill announced Britain's return to the gold standard at the prewar parity, implying a dollar-sterling exchange rate of $4.86 to £1. The restored regime, which overvalued sterling by *at least* 10 per cent, was to last just under six years and five months.

Keynes reacted with a pamphlet, *The Economic Consequences of Mr. Churchill*,[20] which, using the system of analysis of the *Tract*, attacked the assumptions of the decision. It looked at the effects of the decision on the coal industry in particular, concluding that the pressure on miners' wages stemmed directly from the return to gold. As he summed it up:

> They [the miners] are the victims of the economic juggernaut. They represent in the flesh the "fundamental adjustments" engineered by the Treasury and the Bank of England to satisfy the impatience of the City fathers to bridge the "moderate gap" between $4.40 and $4.86. *They* (and others to follow) are the "moderate sacrifice" still necessary to ensure the stability of the gold standard. The plight of the coal miners is the first, but not—unless we are very lucky —the last, of the economic consequences of Mr. Churchill. . . .
>
> The gold standard, with its dependence on pure chance, its faith in "automatic adjustments," and its general regardlessness of social detail, is an essential emblem and idol of those who sit on the top tier of the machine. I think they are immensely rash in their regardlessness, in their vague optimism and comfortable belief that nothing really serious ever happens.

[20] Published in the United States as *The Economic Consequences of the Sterling Parity* (1925; it appears in full in *JMK*, IX).

Nine times out of ten, nothing really serious does happen—merely a little distress to individuals or to groups. But we run a risk of the tenth time (and are stupid into the bargain), if we continue to apply the principles of an economics which was worked out on the hypothesis of *laissez faire* and free competition, to a society which is rapidly abandoning these hypotheses. (*JMK*, IV, 223–24)

However, at the time he was writing those words, Keynes was already beginning to move beyond the Marshallian assumptions of the *Tract*. For in June 1924 he had begun what was to become—after many drafts and redrafts and interruptions for controversy on matters of policy, particularly the monetary policy that followed from the gold standard decision of 1925, and after the composition, for his private amusement, of a substantial history of ancient currency systems—*A Treatise on Money*.[21] As his work on the *Treatise* progressed, changes in view from the analysis of the *Tract* began to creep into his contributions to discussions of policy. These changes were to prove important in the 1930s.

[21] Although scholars in the field in Cambridge urged Keynes to publish his work on ancient currencies, he refused to on the grounds that it represented a result of his hobby and he did not publish such things. Modern scholars consider it still of sufficient interest, and it will appear in *JMK*, in the volume entitled *Social, Political and Literary Writings*.

The Period of Transition, 1925–31

iv

The years surrounding the preparation of the
Treatise were transitional for Keynes in many
respects. In August 1925, after living with her
for some time, he married Lydia Lopokova of the
Diaghilev ballet.[1] The result was somewhat
greater distance from the rest of Bloomsbury:
"they had now become a delightful recreation
instead of being the main background of his
life."[2] With his marriage, Keynes took a lease
on Tilton, a farmhouse at Firle in Sussex, and
he came to divide his life roughly as follows:
London during the week, Cambridge for long
weekends during term, and Tilton for vacations.

[1] To judge from contemporary press cuttings pre-
served by his mother, the marriage was as widely
reported in England and abroad as many recent
events in the film world, with large notices and
pictures.
[2] R. Harrod, *The Life of John Maynard Keynes*,
p. 369.

He also visited Russia for the first time, became even more involved in Liberal party politics and policy formulation, and took a much more active part in industrial affairs. For economists, however, and probably for history, *A Treatise on Money* takes precedence.

Keynes spent six years and two months on the *Treatise*. During this period his ideas were continually changing, and traces of many stages in his development lie in the published version like sloughed-off snake-skins. Nevertheless, despite the fact that, as Keynes put it in the preface, "it represents a collection of material rather than a finished work," the book is a very significant part of his work as an economist.

During the period of the *Treatise*'s composition, Cambridge monetary theory was, in many respects, in its most active phase. For, while Keynes worked at the *Treatise*, Dennis Robertson, one of Keynes's earliest pupils, was, in *Banking Policy and the Price Level* (1926),[3] bringing to the attention of English economists the importance of the distinction between decisions to save and decisions to invest, using the latter in the sense of the acquisition of fixed or working capital goods rather than financial assets, while A. C. Pigou was extending his earlier work in *Industrial Fluctuations* (1927). At the same time, a generation of younger economists—Joan Robinson, Richard Kahn, Piero Sraffa —were coming to exercise an influence, although in monetary matters in this period it was confined to discussion rather than publication. This generation, the

[3] Keynes was intimately involved in the development of the ideas in this book, as his surviving papers and Robertson's comment that in chapters V and VI "neither of us now knows how much the ideas therein contained is his and how much mine" clearly indicate. Mention should also be made of Robertson's classic introduction to monetary theory, *Money* (1922 and 1928), and *A Study of Industrial Fluctuation* (1915).

first purely post-Marshallian generation in Cambridge, was to become very important in Keynes's development as a monetary economist after 1930, but traces of their influence already started to show earlier.

During the same period, outside events provided food for thought. In the United States, the Federal Reserve System after 1922 seemed to be showing the world that monetary management could succesfully achieve price stability with economic expansion. At the same time, the slow, creaking, and eventually unsuccessful adjustment of the British economy to the overvaluation of sterling in 1925 raised questions as to the channels through which monetary influences made their effects felt and the various possible functions of monetary management—where it was and was not an effective policy instrument. It was probably this interaction of intellectual and external stimuli that lay behind the *Treatise*, perhaps Keynes's most complete published integration of matters of theory and policy.

At the center of the *Treatise*, as of the *Tract*, is the question of price stability. However, in the *Treatise*, with his concern for matters of policy, Keynes attempted to explore the dynamics of the price level, only dimly perceived in the formulation of the cash-balances quantity equation of the *Tract*, with its single consumption price level and its relatively aggregative treatment of monetary influences. In doing so, he produced a book that looks in two directions—back to his Marshallian inheritance with its methods, assumptions, and particular concerns, and forward to some of the concerns of *The General Theory of Employment, Interest and Money*, published five and a half years later.

The *Treatise* echoed earlier work in the field in a number of its basic assumptions. First, it continued to assume that money was neutral, in that changes in financial variables did not affect the long-term equilibrium positions of the real variables in the economy. As Keynes summed it up at the end of the book: "Monetary theory, when all is said and done, is little more than a vast elaboration of the truth that 'it all comes out in the wash'" (*JMK*, VI, 366). Despite this basic long-term assumption, the opposite was shown to be the case again and again throughout the actual analysis of the book. Second, the formal logic of the theoretical segments of the book assumed a fixed, "full employment" level of output in the economy with the whole adjustment to monetary disturbances taking place through price changes. As we shall see, when Richard Kahn convinced Keynes of the existence of this basic assumption in the book, this proved to be a major factor causing Keynes to abandon the work and begin to try and reformulate his ideas yet again, with important results. Nevertheless, in his nonformal discussions of the real world, Keynes concerned himself with changes in both prices and output. Even when he did so, however, he tended to assume that there were forces in the system tending to push it back to full employment in the short term. The only case in which he seems to have implied that the situation might be otherwise came in one of his historical case studies: in discussing the events of the depression of the 1890s, he allowed that the appropriate solution was not monetary and suggested that "nothing but strenuous measures on the part of the Government [in the form of public works] could have been successful" (*JMK*, VI, 151).

Working on the basis of these presuppositions, in the *Treatise* Keynes was in many respects taking the Marshallian cash-balances–quantity equation and elaborating it. A large part of the book was concerned with taking the total stock of money and the aggregate velocity of circulation and breaking them into their constituent parts, so that they would become more amenable for use by policy-makers. Bank deposits, for example, were broken down into income deposits, business deposits, and savings deposits, each with its separate velocity. However, in so separating out the types of deposits and the determinants of their behavior, Keynes recognized that it was impossible in practice to measure the magnitude of the new variables with any accuracy. Thus "the 'quantity theory' was transformed into what may be more properly called a 'quality theory,' as it could at the best be used only for purposes of general 'qualitative' analysis of changes in money and prices."[4] In his attempt to flesh out the quantity theory and make it useful for policy, Keynes also had to face the problem of defining the appropriate price levels for the various nominal quantities in the equation. This explains the *Treatise*'s Book II, with its long and intricate discussion of price indices, standards of purchasing power, the diffusion of the influences affecting prices through the various components of the over-all price level with its delightfully apt analogy,[5] and the various principles for the construction of index numbers. It also prepared the way for the development of his "Fundamental Equations" that occupy the heart of his pure theory.

Since 1930, social accounting has made such strides that contemporary economists coming to the *Treatise* for the first time find that they have to reorient themselves to work within Keynes's analysis, for his definitions of income, earnings, profits, and savings all have meanings that differ from the modern usage in almost every introductory textbook treatment. Once over this hurdle, however, they often find in the Fundamental

---

[4] E. Eshag, *From Marshall to Keynes: An Essay on the Monetary Theory of the Cambridge School*, p. 23.
[5] "The effect of moving a kaleidoscope on the coloured pieces of glass within is almost a better metaphor for the influence of monetary changes on price levels" (*JMK*, V, p. 81).

Equations a remarkable engine of analysis which eschews the comparative statics of Keynes's earlier and later work in favour of a more flexible analysis of sequences of events—one which, moreover, takes in a wide range of variables, including several price and cost levels, several alternative breakdowns of the level of output, and both anticipated and realized magnitudes. It is this richness in the *Treatise* that has led several recent commentators to reappraise its usefulness and to come to the conclusion that, despite its flaws, it is much superior to Keynes's later work in its analysis of such things as inflationary situations.

The doctrine of the Fundamental Equations rested on a distinction between investment (or capital outlay) and saving. Keynes, unlike his predecessors (other than Robertson), held that the two, undertaken by differing groups of people for different reasons, need not be equal and that their inequality would in the short period move the economic system toward boom or slump, inflation or deflation. His analysis began with the observation that money incomes are earned by producers of both consumer and capital goods but that only the former come forward for current consumption. If all who earned money spent only a proportion of their incomes equal to the share of consumer goods in total output, all would be well and the system would remain in equilibrium. If, however, the proportion of income spent on consumer goods differed from their share in total output, the producers of such goods, Keynes argued, would experience unexpected[6] increments or decrements of profit from the level at which they would be happy to continue with the existing state of affairs. These un-

[6] In talking about unanticipated windfall profits and losses, Keynes made a serious error subsequently exploited by Gunnar Myrdal. For the fundamental equations work equally well whether or not the profits and losses are foreseen.

expected changes in profit would result in changes in business investment as businessmen altered the composition of their output in response to the signals of the market. The upshot would be changes in output and employment in the short term, with prices following afterward.

The above only touches on the bare bones of the *Treatise* model. In the book there are also a fully developed model of the financial system, notable for its emphasis on what one might call the channels of monetary change; an integrated and well-developed model of the external sector of the economy; a useful classification of types of inflation or deflation in terms of their origins; and several precursors of theoretical constructs that were to prove important in the *General Theory*. Notable among these are much fuller discussion of the motives for holding wealth in the form of money as opposed to securities, which begin to emphasize the role of stocks of outstanding assets in the determination of the terms on which one would acquire new assets; the beginnings of an attempt to bring expectations into theories of the operation of the economy, both as regards the holding of outstanding assets and businessmen's decisions to invest in new plant and equipment; and the beginnings of an effort to understand business investment decisions. Added to these was a wealth of empirical information, for in developing new tools Keynes always kept an eye on their applicability to the contemporary world and contemporary policy, and, where possible, provided estimates of orders of magnitude.

Some of the analytical contributions of the *Treatise* become clearer if one turns to the effects on the book of Keynes's views on the role of monetary policy, for as composition proceeded Keynes's advice altered. These are best summarized as follows:

1. The explicit shift to a savings-investment frame-

work of analysis increased the importance of the long-term rate of interest. In the *Treatise*, as well, the distinction between the "natural" and the market rate of interest made its appearances. Such a distinction, hinted at by Marshall,[7] had existed in the work of Knut Wicksell, a Swedish predecessor of Keynes, but the *Treatise* formulation seems to have (as was usual in Keynes's work as an economist) evolved independently of a knowledge of the literature. In the *Treatise*, the natural rate of interest was the equilibrium rate at which saving and capital outlay would be equal, with no forces leading to changes in prices. On the other hand, the market rate, which influenced businessmen's investment decisions, was the result of the public's preferences concerning the form in which they would hold their assets (cash, savings deposits, or securities) and the policy of the banking system. Divergences between the two rates would lead to pressure toward inflation or deflation in the system, as capital goods looked cheap or dear in relation to the price of securities.

2. The emphasis on the long-term rate was coupled with a diminished emphasis on the effects of changes in short-term rates of interest, especially as Keynes had come to believe (perhaps partially as a result of his increased knowledge of practical finance during the 1920s) that the volume of investment in working capital was relatively insensitive to changes in the short-term rate of interest.

3. Given his own previous emphasis on changes in Bank rate, the fact that most of his contemporaries placed great emphasis on it, and the fact that it remained perhaps the most readily usable instrument of monetary policy, Keynes, with his new emphasis on the importance of the long-term rate of interest, was faced

[7] See above p. 46.

with the problem of explaining how changes in short-term rates of interest could affect the long rate, which historically had been stable relative to the large swings in short rates. Hence he developed a theory of what economists know as the term structure of interest rates, a problem not extensively discussed previously, and showed much concern with the "conventional" expectational factors impeding the flexibility of the long rate in the short period.

4. The *Treatise*, with its focus on the various uses of funds and its theory of the market rate of interest that centered on patterns of asset-holding, naturally saw much greater importance in supplies of credit for particular uses rather than simply the supply of credit as a whole.

5. In developing the distinction between what he called income and profit inflations (or deflations), Keynes introduced explicitly a case where monetary policy, because its results came indirectly (depending as they did on the effects of increased unemployment on money wage bargaining), was "singularly ill adapted" —to achieving a reduction in incomes.

6. In the *Treatise*, Keynes shifted his ground from the doctrine of the *Tract* and accepted the desirability of an international standard of value. He took great pains to elaborate the pros and cons of such a standard, but having accepted the case for it, largely on the grounds of the importance of foreign lending, he proceeded to recommend a standard that would be an improvement on the gold standard. This standard would be managed by an international central bank committed to keeping the standard of value stable in terms of the prices of sixty commodities that moved in international trade (*JMK*, VI, 351–52). The scheme provided for some safeguards for national autonomy in monetary

policy through such devices as a wider range of exchange-rate fluctuation around exchange parities, which would remain perpetually fixed.

7. The major disadvantage of *any* international standard with perpetually fixed exchange rates and freedom for international capital movements was the dilemma it could pose for an individual country whose domestic circumstances called for a monetary policy different from that which adherence to the standard implied. The dilemma would become particularly acute for a nation whose level of efficiency wages (money wages adjusted for productivity) proved too high to allow it full employment at the existing set of international interest rates, although these rates might be appropriate for the system as a whole. In these circumstances, the nation's monetary authorities could not use monetary policy to preserve full employment, because lower interest rates would result in capital outflows and a loss of gold and foreign-exchange reserves, which would eventually force them to reverse the policy or abandon the standard. Nor was it desirable that they should attempt to use monetary policy to reduce money wages, as this was a long, slow, and socially wasteful process. However, there was a reserve weapon available: through loan-financed public-works or capital-development schemes (with an accommodating credit policy to allow for the expanded need for working capital) employment could expand at the existing rate of interest. However, this was a "special case" for public works. In the general case, monetary policy concentrating on the long-term rate of interest and the adjustment of the supply of credit for the varying needs of the economy was the appropriate solution to the problems of aggregate economic management.

The years surrounding the final stages of writing and publication of the *Treatise* were dramatic ones for an economist heavily interested in policy as Keynes was. And 1928 saw the beginnings of the final, spectacular stage of the great Wall Street stock-exchange boom of the late 1920s and considerable controversy as to its implications. The year 1929 brought a revision of the German reparations settlement of 1924 and a British general election in which the Liberal party, as part of an attempt to shift the ground of debate away from traditional issues and thus ensure its survival as a major political force, campaigned on a program of capital development and environmental improvement. The next year, the first of the great slump, saw Keynes an active member of the Macmillan Committee on Finance and Industry and an influential figure in the Prime Minister's new Economic Advisory Council and its many committees. During the following year, as the slump continued to deepen, the painfully reconstructed post-war international financial system collapsed as a liquidity crisis swept Western Europe. And Britain, already in serious balance-of-payments difficulties at the 1925 exchange rate and unable to stand the strain of acting as an international banker in the circumstances, left the gold standard, following a desperate deflationary budget and the exhaustion of her foreign reserves.

Throughout the period, Keynes tended to apply the relevant portions of the *Treatise* to the situation. Thus, in discussing the implications of the stock-exchange boom, he made use of the *Treatise*'s distinction between various uses of credit and argued that the Federal Reserve should not treat the boom as evidence of inflation which required tight money to end it. The Federal Reserve might even have to increase the supply of credit to prevent deflationary pressures arising from firms whose normal sources of credit had dried up as a result of the diversion of cash balances from the industrial circulation to security speculation.

Similarly, in newspaper articles, in a magnificent political pamphlet entitled *Can Lloyd George Do It?* (written with Hubert Henderson and supporting the Liberal election program of 1929), in eight days of private evidence to the Macmillan Committee, and in memoranda to the Economic Advisory Council and its committees, Keynes used the "special case" of the *Treatise* to deal with the problems of the British economy under the overvalued 1925 exchange rate, advocating public works as the solution to British unemployment until the opportunity came to get the long-term rate of interest down to an appropriate level. As his advocacy of public works developed, Keynes turned to consider more thoroughly the balance-of-payments implications of the increased demand for imports that would follow the increased employment and income resulting from public-works schemes. He proceeded to advocate restrictions on overseas lending and, reversing his earlier free-trade position, a revenue tariff with provisions for an export subsidy to ease the situation.

On the other hand, when talking in June 1931 in the United States, a country with a very small overseas sector and an exchange rate he believed appropriate to her economic circumstances, Keynes followed the general case of the *Treatise*. As he put it:

I think the argument for public works in this country [the United States] is much weaker than it is in Great Britain. In Great Britain I have for a long time past agitated very strongly for a public works program, and my argument has been that we are such a center of an international system that we cannot operate on the rate of interest, because if we tried to force the rate of interest down, there is too much lending, and we lose our gold. . . .

In this country you haven't a problem of that kind. Here you can function as though you were a closed

system, and . . . for such a system I would use my first
method operating on the long-term rate of interest.[8]

Finally, in discussing the proposed "solution" to the
German reparations problem, Keynes turned to what
one might regard another variant of the "special case."
Up to 1929, he argued, German prices and costs had
become adjusted to a situation where overseas borrowing, which could not last, effectively covered reparations
payments. If such borrowing ceased and Germany had
to effect a transfer of reparations payments abroad, her
exports must rise and/or her imports fall. Such changes,
in a world of fixed exchange rates, carried with them the
implication that German efficiency wages would have
to fall below the level at which they would have stood
if borrowing had continued. The only available policy
instrument, monetary policy, if used to improve the
balance-of-payments position would produce domestic
deflation, a process which would create economic and
political instability in Germany—instability which would
have important implications elsewhere in the international economy. Keynes's opposition to the new reparations proposal logically followed.

The consistency between Keynes's theory and his
policy advice was remarkably strong, to put it mildly.
If further confirmation is necessary, Keynes's reactions
to the financial crisis of the late summer of 1931 and
its aftermath provide an ideal test case.

The 1931 financial crisis affected both the gold-
standard system, as reconstructed after 1918, and
Britain's possible role in the international economy. In
the light of events, Keynes's view of policy possibilities
began to change even before Britain left gold. For the

[8] N. W. Harris Memorial Foundation, *Reports of Round
Tables: Unemployment as a World Problem* (mimeo.) (Chicago, 1931), p. 303.

impending collapse of the post-1918 system, sparked
off by deflation-induced financial collapses in central
Europe, meant that the way was open for a replacement,
that international concerns could again become important subjects of efforts at persuasion. Keynes began to
prepare the ground for a new system through hints in
articles and explicit advice in letters to the Prime Minister. As well, when Britain left gold on September 21,
1931, and the exchange value of sterling could adjust
to make British efficiency wages internationally competitive, she ceased to be a "special case" in the *Treatise*
sense. Keynes, in a letter to *The Times* (and a later
article in *The Sunday Express*), immediately withdrew
his proposal for a tariff and announced that "the immediate question for attention is not a tariff but the currency question" (*JMK*, IX, 243–44). The Treasury—
with a consideration for the views of economists writing
to that newspaper that it has perhaps sensibly, subsequently abandoned, responded by asking Keynes for
his views on the matter.

Keynes's reply (which he also sent to the Prime Minister, who circulated it to, and made Keynes a member
of, his Advisory Committee on Financial Questions)
caused extensive discussion in the Treasury. In turn it
drew from the Treasury a reply that eventually went to
the cabinet in March 1932 as the outline of Britain's
short-term post-gold-standard policy and, as such, formed
a part of the story of the origins of the cheap-money
policy that was to be dominant in Britain until 1951.

Keynes's memorandum advocated the convening of a
conference of countries which had linked their currencies to sterling through a gold-exchange standard regime
before 1931 and/or had followed sterling's departure
from gold in September, in order that they might adopt
among themselves the international standard of value
recommended in the last chapter of the *Treatise*. This

standard would be managed so as to restore an index of
the prices of the main commodities in international
trade to its 1929 level and thence keep it steady by
means of the Bank of England's setting appropriate
weekly buying and selling prices for gold (and hence
the range for exchange-rate fluctuations) along lines
outlined not only in the *Treatise* but also in the *Tract*.
Although the adoption of this standard, as the *Treatise*
recognized, would not eliminate the possible conflict for
Britain between internal and external stability, since the
exchange rate chosen for sterling in the scheme might
differ from that which would best further Britain's
short-term interests, the difference would not be large
and the return to prosperity in the associated countries
would encourage British exports. The scheme would be
a "good working compromise between the ideals of exchange stability and price stability."

Turning to Britain's domestic situation, the memorandum also remained mainstream *Treatise*. Keynes *did not*
mention public works. To encourage recovery from the
slump through domestic measures, the authorities should
use interest-rate policy—encourage, yet wait for, conditions suitable for the conversion of the major block of
World War I government debt which dominated the
contemporary long-term rate of interest to a level 40
per cent lower. In fact, he did not strongly advocate
public-works schemes in British, or any other, conditions
for the better part of a year after the memorandum.
When he did so, Keynes was already on the way to
formulating a new set of ideas—those which we now
associate with his *General Theory*.

The Years of the
General Theory, 1931–37

In April 1932, just fifteen months after the publication of *A Treatise On Money*, Keynes concluded the preface to the Japanese translations as follows:

> I should add . . . that after a year and a half of further reflection and after having had the advantage of much criticism and discussion of my theories, I have naturally made many *addenda* and *corrigenda* in what follows. It is not, however, my intention to revise the existing text of this *Treatise* in the near future. I propose, rather, to publish a short book of a purely theoretical character, extending and correcting the theoretical basis of my views as set forth . . . below. (*JMK*, V, xxvii)

In fact, he had started the long process of "work-it out all over again" some time before.

Why did he abandon the *Treatise* so quickly?

To understand the reasons, we must look at the discussions that followed the publication of the book. These discussions took place on three levels:

To begin with, the book naturally received extensive reviews and was the subject of comments. From the reviews and published comments, particularly those by F. A. Hayek and D. H. Robertson, and from discussions with economists such as A. C. Pigou, Keynes came to realize that he had not made himself absolutely clear in the text and, moreover, had made a serious error in the specification of the Fundamental Equations for the purposes of handling movements of output that often made them inconsistent with his verbal exposition of the processes studied.

In August 1930, just before the *Treatise* was finished, Richard Kahn, inspired by *Can Lloyd George Do It?*, developed a framework for analyzing the relationship between the direct employment resulting from public works and their ultimate effect on the economy (the multiplier). He presented this in an early draft form in September to the Economic Advisory Council's Committee of Economists, of which Keynes was chairman and Kahn joint secretary. In the ensuing months, in collaboration with Colin Clark and James Meade, he elaborated his early draft and worked out its implications much more fully before publishing it in the *Economic Journal* for June 1931 under the title "The Relation of Home Investment to Unemployment."

Most important, 1931 saw the beginning (and end) of the Circus, a group of younger Cambridge economists, including Joan and Austin Robinson, Richard Kahn, James Meade, Piero Sraffa, and such research students and undergraduates as could pass the stiff oral examination required for joining the seminar; these young economists set to work to digest, to understand, and, inevitably, to criticize the *Treatise*. After a term and a half of formal meetings of the Circus (and perhaps another two months of informal ones) Meade returned to Oxford following his year in Cambridge, at such a stage in his own thinking that he claims he was not surprised by the form developments took in the course of the next few years.[1]

These three strands of discussion raised some major points of difficulty:

1. The formal error in the specification of the Fundamental Equations, which Hayek and others had pointed out, meant that the verbal discussions concerning movements in output were inconsistent with the Equations.

2. In the formal exposition of the book, discrepancies between saving and investment resulted in changes in the price levels of investment goods, consumption goods, or, with a lag, labor, which then affected profit levels.[2] This tended to imply a fixed national output, with adjustment occurring only through price-level changes, and as a general theory it was inadequate, as the events of 1930–31 were making painfully clear. Toward this conclusion, Kahn's multiplier article was the primary impulse, for it focused on the shapes of the supply curves for investment and consumption goods. Using this formulation, Kahn realized clearly that the *Treatise* equations were a limiting case—that of complete inelasticity of output in response to demand changes—which was not really relevant to the conditions of 1930–31, when British unemployment averaged between 2 and 3 million.

[1] We know a fair bit about the mechanics of the Circus. However, very little written evidence of their deliberations survives. What does survive, plus an agreed note by the surviving participants as to what they discussed, appears in *JMK*, XIII, 203–207, 337–43.

[2] The best example of this is the Widow's Cruse (see *JMK*, V, 125). The mistake became known as the Widow's Cruse Fallacy.

3. Another contribution to the Circus also came from Kahn, who, in collaboration with Meade, evolved Mr. Meade's Relation," providing for a clear statement of the sources of the resources for additional investment when the supply of output was not completely inelastic.

4. Finally, Kahn attacked the ascription by Keynes in the Fundamental Equations of different determinants for the price level of consumption goods (p) and investment goods (p'). In two notes in April 1931 he developed the argument which Joan Robinson was to use in an article published in 1933, and demonstrated that "if one clears the decks of your special definitions [of savings] it is surely clear that p and p' *are* directly related except in the most extreme case when no part of profits is devoted to consumption." Thus the difference between consumption and investment was only one of degree and Keynes was "sheltering . . . behind the arbitrary asymmetry of [his] definition of savings."[3] For, according to Kahn, if p' rose, p would rise. This also implied that if investment rose, consumption would rise also, thus putting the Circus, and, after much thought and many attempts to refute Kahn's point, Keynes, on the verge of what was to become the *General Theory*.

These criticisms had their effect on Keynes, as is clear from several sources. First, he began, quite early on, to try and recast his analysis more explicitly in terms of changes in output. This process had certainly started in a very preliminary way before the formal meetings of the Circus. Second, even when basically arguing the *Treatise* type of case, as in Chicago in June 1931 (*JMK*, XIII, 343–67), he also began to pay more attention to output changes and to drop hints of the possibility of the system coming to rest in a situation of less than full

[3] Both of these quotations come from one of Kahn's later attempts to drive home the point to Keynes (see *JMK*, XIII, 219, 203–207).

employment—something the *Treatise* had not allowed for except in the "special case." However, before looking in detail at the ways in which Keynes reached the position of the *General Theory* and the effects of reaching it on the evolution of his policy advice, it is, perhaps, more useful to jump ahead of ourselves and look at the final result.

The *General Theory* itself, for all its flashes of brilliance and elegance, is perhaps the most obscurely written of Keynes's contributions to economics. Partially, this is a reflection of his "long struggle of escape" (*JMK*, VII, xxiii) from earlier modes of analysis and his constant fretting, especially after his experience with the *Treatise*, over matters of definition. It is also a reflection of the form of analysis Keynes adopted. After working his intuitive ideas out in the sequential framework of the *Treatise*, which is so well adapted for dealing with disequilibrium situations, Keynes recognized that the definitional problems involved in dealing with slices of time of different lengths inherent in the method would detract from his over-all purpose. And as he told J. R. Hicks in June 1935, "I deliberately refrain in my forthcoming book from pursuing anything very far, my object being to press home as forcibly as possibly certain fundamental opinions—and no more."

Thus he adopted a form of comparative static analysis that is basically less well suited for describing disequilibrium situations but is extremely useful for getting his message across to nonspecialists. On top of these difficulties are the usual problems of the "Cambridge didactic style" with its hiding of awkward complications from plain view, the regular intrusions into the argument of Keynes the social philosopher and prophet, and Keynes's very Marshallian habit of taking the argument one step at a time in a manner that looks like unidirectional causation but is not. Nevertheless, one cannot help but marvel at how much he managed to pack into the book's 384 pages.

Looking at the book as a whole—and supplementing what one finds there with his few subsequent published and unpublished replies to comments and criticisms (these appear together in *JMK*, XIV)—it is probably best to begin by noting the points where Keynes broke from past practice and doctrine:

1. The book focused primarily on output and employment rather than on prices. This did not mean that Keynes did not devote any attention to price changes, but rather that he did so after keeping the matter in the background during the main chapters where he developed the building blocks of his new theory.

2. Rather than arising in asides, as in the *Treatise*, uncertainty dominated the *General Theory*. Keynes explained what he meant by uncertainty:

> By "uncertain" knowledge . . . I do not mean merely to distinguish what is known for certain from what is only probable. The game of roulette is not subject, in this sense, to uncertainty; nor is the prospect of a Victory bond [or in modern usage a lottery ticket] being drawn. Or, again, the expectation of life is only slightly uncertain. Even the weather is only moderately uncertain. The sense in which I am using the term is that in which the prospect of a European war is uncertain, or the price of copper and the rate of interest twenty years hence, or the obsolescence of a new invention, or the position of private wealth owners in the social system of 1970. About these matters there is no scientific basis on which to form any calculable probability whatever. We simply do not know. Nevertheless, the necessity for action and decision compels us as practical men to overlook this awkward fact. . . .
>
> How do we manage in such circumstances to behave in a manner which saves our faces as rational eco-

nomic men. We have devised for the purpose a variety of techniques. . . .

Now a practical theory of the future based on these . . . principles has certain marked characteristics. In particular, being based on so flimsy a foundation, it is subject to sudden and violent changes. The practice of calmness and immobility, of certainty and security, suddenly breaks down. New plans and hopes will, without warning, take charge of human conduct. . . . All these pretty, polite techniques, made for a well panelled board room and a nicely regulated market are likely to collapse. At all times the vague panic fears and equally vague and unreasoned hopes are not really lulled, and lie but a little way below the surface.

. . . I accuse the classical economic theory of being itself one of those pretty, polite techniques which tries to deal with the present by abstracting from the fact that we know very little about the future. (*JMK*, XIV, 113–15; see also VII, 148–53)

3. In an uncertain world moving through time, Keynes argued, money plays a peculiar role—a role ignored in the frequently timeless equilibrium world of traditional theory. The role of money reflects several characteristics of the real world: in normal circumstances[4] legally enforceable contracts are denominated in money; in most markets in the economy money, rather than goods, buys goods; prices, expressed in terms of money, are the primary sources of information for economic actors. In the real world, Keynes argued, individuals desiring to avoid current commitments owing to uncertainty as to future developments are more likely

[4] Of course, if the monetary system exhibits wild instability the roles of money may change. But such instability, as historical experience indicates, must be very extreme—e.g., hyperinflationary—before the normal roles of money disintegrate.

to hold money or money substitutes rather than any other asset. Thus changing views as to the future will affect the demand for money.

4. Given the uncertainty of the world, Keynes suggested that the "conventions" accepted by economic actors in their day-to-day behavior could include some prices. As a result, prices might be relatively sticky in the short period and the economic system's reactions to short-period disturbances might involve changes in the volume of such things as output and employment.

5. Given the central role of money in an uncertain world, Keynes argued, it is not neutral in the sense that changes in its quantity have no effect on the equilibrium positions of the real variables in the economic system, the position adopted by his orthodox predecessors; it is not a veil behind which the real variables interact, and it is not inessential to the final result.

6. In the *General Theory*, Keynes argued that the normal assumption of his predecessors (as well as himself, he admitted, in books such as the *Treatise*), that the economic system automatically tends only toward full employment, was mistaken and the economic system could be stable at less than full employment. Hence his claim to have produced a general theory in which the traditional full-employment theory represented a special case.

7. Keynes also suggested that his *General Theory* represented an integration of the traditional theory of relative prices (or value theory to economists) and monetary theory, for it linked individual supply and demand behavior with aggregate monetary behavior. Successors, including such followers as Roy Harrod, initially discounted this claim. Others thought it invalid because they could construct models with classical tools and assumptions that integrated the two and reached "Keynesian" conclusions with a few strategically chosen

assumptions as to the rigidity of particular prices. However, recent work by economists of several schools has indicated persuasively that by ignoring uncertainty and thus the asset demand rather than the mere transactions role of money, these theorists in the older tradition have ignored or evaded the heart of the problems raised by Keynes. Although, as yet, no one claims to have successfully integrated monetary and value theory, the palm goes to Keynes for having seen the basis of the problem.

The above represents only a very general catalogue of Keynes's breaks with the past. In making these breaks and in presenting his model of the economic system, Keynes concentrated on a series of building blocks in a short-period framework of analysis. This framework, plus his exclusion of international trade and investment from the model (also a departure from the *Treatise*), swept many problems under the carpet, but, linked with the vision suggested in the more general catalogue above, it has proved remarkably useful and influential.

The first building block in Keynes's system, in which decisions to produce output, invest, and hold money depended on expectations of an uncertain future, was the consumption-income relationship, which had been implicit in the work of Marshall and in Keynes's own earlier writings on the relationship between changes in interest rates and changes in savings. Put briefly, it suggested that in the short period changes in consumption were determined primarily by changes in income but that, in normal circumstances, consumption changes by less than income. In his discussion of this relationship, labeled the "propensity to consume," Keynes allowed for most of the factors that would affect the form of the relationship and its position over time,[5] but, when in

---

[5] Changes in tax rates, corporate savings practices, changes in relative prices and market structures, and so on.

his presentation he came to set it out, he tended to keep these in the background and concentrate on a generalized, "psychological," portmanteau relationship. He also tended to assume that as incomes rose over time, increments in consumption would take up increasingly smaller portions of the rises. This nonproportional form of consumption function lay behind his frequently expressed view that economic growth at normal levels, continued over a couple of generations, would raise incomes to such a level that investment demands would be satiated and society could settle down to worry about more important problems than the economic one. This, plus his conception of the good life, also lay behind his desire to reach "bliss" as soon as possible by encouraging changes in investment rather than consumption to maintain full employment.

The first building block, the consumption function, led on to the second—the multiplier. For, if the supply of output was elastic (i.e., the economy was working at less than full capacity), then increases in investment (say, in the form of public-works expenditure), would lead to an expansion of income until, in the new situation, the amount saved from the increased income would be equal to the amount of new investment. The expansion of income would be a multiple greater than one of the increased investment so long as the whole increment of income was not saved; i.e., the multiplier's size depended on the propensity to consume marginal increments in income.

The third building block in the system was the demand of businessmen and others for new capital goods (plant, machinery, houses, etc.), or for what Keynes called investment. Here, more than in decisions to produce current output, expectations moved to the center of the stage, since decisions to acquire capital assets depended on a comparison between the expected returns from acquiring an asset, now, to produce a stream of output in the future, and the current cost of the asset. The expected returns themselves depended on such factors as future levels of demand, and/or future costs of production both for the particular enterprise and for its likely competitors, which might, of course, use later technologies or buy inputs at different future prices. The costs of any investment were themselves known, although they might change over the short period when demand for investment goods changed. As the returns from any investment were expected to accrue over a period of years in the future, while its cost was known, there must be a rate of discount which would make the two comparable. This rate of discount Keynes christened the marginal efficiency of capital. He then suggested that businessmen would carry their investment in new capital goods to the point at which the marginal efficiency of capital equaled the cost of funds for undertaking the investment (in the shorthand terms of the economist, the rate of interest).

The fourth building block in the system was Keynes's theory of the rate of interest. Starting from his Marshallian background, Keynes began with an examination of the motives for holding money, which, following convention, he assumed did not yield interest. These motives he broke down into the transactions motive (i.e., the need to hold money for transaction purposes between paydays, etc.), the precautionary motive (i.e., the need to hold money against unforeseen contingencies), and the speculative motive. This last motive needs more discussion, for, through two brilliant simplifications, Keynes set it at the heart of his theory of the rate of interest. The first simplification was to assume that the precautionary and transactions motives could be separated from the speculative motive and lumped together, and then, having lumped them together, to argue that the demand for money to met these motives was mainly a function of the income level. The second simplification was so to define money for the purposes of analysis that transactors could choose only between money and long-term bonds, all other securities being either money or, in the case of shares, proxies for capital assets themselves.[6] Now one of the characteristics of long-term bonds is that small changes in the interest rate lead to large changes in price. With a perpetual bond such as a British Government Consol with a face value of £100 yielding 10 per cent per annum, if the rate of interest rises to 11 per cent the price will fall to £90. Thus if an asset holder, faced with the decision to hold money or bonds, expects the interest rate to rise by more than one per cent in the next year, he would have as much incentive to hold cash as to buy bonds.[7] Seizing on this relationship, Keynes then went on to suggest that, given future expectations on the part of wealth holders, the rate of interest would have to adjust so as to ensure that all the money not taken up by the transactions and precautionary motives would be held by the public. Such expectations, Keynes realized, might have a strong element of convention in them, so that official policies designed to alter the rate of interest by altering the quantity of money might have little effect, for, as the rate fell away from the conventional rate, the strong expectation that it would return to it in future would mean that asset holders would take up the increase in the speculative motive. Of course, in the model at this point, the dependence of the demand for money on

---

[6] In lumping equities and capital assets together, Keynes's analysis here was much less rich than his own previous analysis in the *Treatise*.
[7] To put it more generally, if he expects the rate of increase in the interest rate to exceed the existing interest rate he would hold cash.

level of income, and hence the implication that changes
in income level would also affect the interest rate within
the limits set by expectations, meant that the system
was determinate, in the sense that every variable was
determined by its interaction with others in the model.

Added to these four basic building blocks were discussions of the determination of prices by the supply
functions of differing components of output, of the
effects of changes in money wages on prices and employment, of the trade cycle, and of the essential prop-
erties of money, not to mention asides on the implications of the theory for the future of capitalist society
and a search for precursors for his ideas.

Having worked through the essential notions of the
General Theory, let us turn back to its creation and the
effects of that creation on Keynes's views of policy,
leaving an over-all assessment of the book to a later
chapter.

You don't mention *effective demand* or, more pre-
cisely, the demand schedule for output as a whole,
except in so far as it is implicit in the multiplier. To
me, the most extraordinary thing, regarded historically, is the complete disappearance of the theory of
the demand and supply for output as a whole, i.e. the
theory of employment, *after* it had been for a quarter
of a century the most discussed thing in economics.
One of the most important transitions for me, after
my *Treatise on Money* had been published, was suddenly realising this. It only came after I had enunci-
ated to myself the psychological law that, when income increases, the gap between income and consumption will increase,—a conclusion of vast importance to my own thinking but not apparently, expressed just like this, to anyone else's. Then, appreciably later, came the notion of interest as being the
meaning of liquidity preference, which became quite

clear in my mind the moment I thought of it. And last of all, after an immense lot of muddling and many drafts, the proper definition of the marginal efficiency of capital linked up one thing with another. (*JMK*, XIV, 84–86)

In this way, at the end of August 1936, Keynes outlined to Roy Harrod the process by which his ideas developed. In doing so, however, he made the composition of the *General Theory* and its system of ideas sound remarkably simple. In actual fact, from the casting of the first doubts on the *Treatise* in the winter and spring of 1931 to the completion of the *General Theory*, the process of creation was much more painful, and much less simple —although it is clear that at every point Keynes's intuition moved ahead of his analysis.

Although hints of the doubts induced by the Circus's work appeared, as we have already noted, in Keynes's lectures at the Harris Foundation in Chicago in the summer of 1931, he appears to have started seriously to move away from the *Treatise* only in the late summer and autumn of 1931. One surviving scrap of correspondence with Richard Kahn, dated September 20, 1931, saw Keynes working clearly in terms of changes in output, rather than in terms of changes in prices as in the *Treatise*, and using a crude income-savings relation to show how equilibrium was perfectly possible at less than full employment. However, at this stage, the analysis and the conclusions were tentative, and it is not surprising that when Britain left the gold standard, Keynes's policy advice, still resting firmly on the general analysis of the *Treatise*, dropped the advocacy of public works characteristic of the "special case" of that book, an advocacy he had pursued for more than three years previously. He did not return to the serious advocacy of public works until late in 1932.

During that year he got himself well into his new set of ideas, at least intuitively. In the spring Keynes gave his first lectures in Cambridge since 1929. Although he retained the title "The Pure Theory of Money," which he had used in 1929 when lecturing from the first proof sheets of the *Treatise*, the content of the lectures had shifted considerably. As far as we can tell from his correspondence with others in Cambridge, they were cast in the *Treatise*'s disequilibrium framework but with movements in output, investment, and consumption, and aggregate supply-and-demand analysis playing an important role. After giving the lectures, during the long summer vacation, Keynes began, as he had told his Japanese readers of the *Treatise*, to work on his new book. At first it seems to have gone fairly quickly, for by September he was able to tell his mother he had written nearly a third of it. From this period, drafts of several chapters, students' lecture notes from the autumn when he lectured under a changed title ("The Monetary Theory of Production"), and a paper of the same title in a *festschrift* for a German professor survive.[8]

From the avialable evidence, it is clear that by the autumn of 1932 Keynes had reached the following conclusions:

1. A monetary economy behaved in a fundamentally different manner from a barter economy or a neutral money economy where money is only a neutral, transitory link in the chain of transaction. For Keynes by 1932, the presence of money in the economy was of crucial importance, since it affected the behavior of *relative* prices, (especially wages and the rate of interest) in disequilibrium conditions, and hence affected

[8] All the material from Keynes's pen directly related to the *General Theory* in this and later periods, supplemented by lecture notes from students, appears in *JMK*, XIII.

the final-equilibrium resting place of the economy after the disturbance in question had passed. This marked a fundamental departure from previous doctrine.

2. In the relationship between income and consumption, changes in consumption followed changes in income by a lesser amount but in the same direction. Keynes had not as yet extracted anything approaching the formal elegance of the multiplier from this view, nor had he really settled on a clearcut definition of income.

3. His conception of liquidity preference related relative desires to hold fixed-interest securities and money (rather than a mixture of equities, fixed-interest securities, and money used in the *Treatise*) to given interest rates.

4. Using a form of aggregate supply-and-demand analysis, he had worked out relationships between the "price complexes" of capital and consumption goods, but he had not as yet boiled down the analysis to the sharpness of the marginal efficiency of capital.

From the autumn of 1932 Keynes appears to have moved more quickly and confidently toward the set of ideas that we associate with the *General Theory*, and his newfound confidence showed in his policy advice.[9] The channels for this advice remained much as before, except that after 1931 the Committee on Economic Information of the Economic Advisory Council, whose meetings and reports Keynes dominated, became an important vehicle for successfully passing his ideas directly into the Whitehall machine.[10] Between November 1932

[9] There are, it is true, traces of his formulation of liquidity preference in his contemporary discussion of the British government's conversion of War Loan from a 5 per-cent to a 3.5 per-cent basis in the summer of 1932, but these are, perhaps, more easily appreciated with hindsight.

[10] For a full discussion of the work of this committee and its influence on policy in the 1930s, see the forthcoming book on the Economic Advisory Council by Susan Howson and

and April 1933, first in Committee on Economic Information Reports and then in three articles in *The Times* (subsequently published as *The Means to Prosperity*; see *JMK*, IX), Keynes returned to the advocacy of public-works policy, not as a remedy for Britain alone but as a general internal remedy for the slump. He provided additional justification for his views in an article called "The Multiplier," which appeared in, of all places, the *New Statesman* on April Fool's Day, 1933, before being included in the American edition of *The Means*. In his approach to public-works policy, Keynes argued that businessmen's expectations had been so shattered by the slump that monetary policy *by itself* could not encourage investment through cheap money, with the result that increased investment in fixed and working capital had to await rather than lead a rise in the level of final demand. Therefore, loan-financed public works would be necessary initially to raise the level of final demand, after which low interest rates would allow private investment to sustain the recovery.[11]

Donald Winch. At this point all the reader needs to know is that the old, formal, full council was one of the victims of the 1931 financial crisis, plus its own impotence, and that the Committee on Economic Information became its successor, lasting until 1939. Its members included Sir Josiah Stamp (a businessman-economist and its chairman), H. D. Henderson, and (after 1935) D. H. Robertson and two Treasury civil servants, Sir Frederick Leith-Ross and Sir Frederick Phillips.

[11] *The Means to Prosperity* also included a suggestion for an international central bank with power to issue its own notes. Although in many respects this was a logical development of ideas in the *Treatise*, it also reflected the attempts of Keynes and H. D. Henderson in the Committee on Economic Information to persuade the British government to propose such a scheme at the forthcoming World Economic Conference. The attempt was not completely successful. Unlike the *Treatise* version, the scheme allowed for changes in exchange rates, thus moving toward the post-1945 Bretton Woods arrangements.

Another indication of Keynes's growing confidence in his ideas was that he began, as was usual, to find predecessors for them. In preparing his *Essays in Biography* for the press during the winter of 1932–33, he revived a 1922 essay on T. R. Malthus, the early nineteenth-century economist, which he had originally prepared for the London Political Economy Club and had read in Cambridge at intervals during the 1920s. Taking the opportunity of the contemporaneous work by Piero Sraffa on Ricardo to revise the essay, at the last possible moment he added passages attributing to Malthus germs of his own recently worked-out views (*JMK*, X).

The Means to Prosperity—with its emphasis on the role of public works in raising the level of final demand to a point where cheap (or, as Keynes continually advocated at the time, cheaper) long-term money, resulting from appropriate monetary and debt-management policies,[12] could act to sustain and further raise the level of private investment—marked the emergence of one strand of the Keynesian policy message eventually embodied in the *General Theory*. Another element, that matters as important as employment policy and the

---

[12] Debt-management policy refers to the authorities' actions concerning the maturity composition of the national debt. Keynes, with his emphasis on the long-term rate of interest, had developed a theory of the relationship between short and long rates in the *Treatise*. As the *General Theory* progressed, the *Treatise* view evolved into an analogue of the theory of liquidity preference where the rates of interest on various maturities became adjusted so as to induce the public to hold these various maturities willingly, given their asset-holding conventions and expectations. In these circumstances, Keynes believed that the existing policy of funding (i.e., increasing the supply of long-term debt and reducing the supply of shorts) pursued by the British authorities tended to raise the rate of interest and hamper recovery. He lost few opportunities to criticize the policy, especially those given by his position as economist-chairman of a major insurance company.

experiments necessary to achieve it made certain elements of "national self-sufficiency" desirable, came at about the same time, as Keynes reverted to his 1930–31 attitude that protection was desirable in certain circumstances.[13] However, the sharpening of the intuitive ideas lying behind this general-policy advice and their presentation in a form fit for his professional colleagues was to take more than two years of further hard work.

The only surviving indication of the state of Keynes's theoretical evolution during the remainder of 1933—beyond a brief note to Joan Robinson concerning his theory of the rate of interest, a promise to his publisher to have his new book ready by mid-1934, and a draft table of contents for a book entitled *The General Theory of Employment*—came in his undergraduate lectures in the autmun. In these, Keynes launched into his substantive theory after certain preliminaries, which included a statement that these lectures embodied a distinct break from those of the past and an attack on A. C. Pigou's recently published *Theory of Unemployment*, which had argued that in pure theory, which Keynes called "classical," money-wage flexibity would preserve full employment in the long run.[14] In present-

[13] "National Self-Sufficiency," *New Statesman and Nation*, 8 and 15 July, 1933. In his biography, Sir Roy Harrod attributes this article in part to Keynes's "revulsion" from the futilities of the World Economic Conference, which President Roosevelt effectively ended on July 3 (p. 446). However, as Keynes delivered the substance of the articles in a lecture in Dublin on April 19, this view seems hard to sustain.

[14] Although Pigou's book was primarily an exercise in pure theory, it did discuss contemporary events. When it came to these, the author did allow for public-works schemes as short-period remedies for unemployment. Here he was only echoing a conclusion that he had held, along with many other economists, since before 1914. Perhaps the cartoon by David Low (reprinted in *JMK*, IX, 337) reflects most accurately the policy consensus in 1933, even if it ignores the disputes over the theory behind it.

ing his own theory, Keynes used the realization problem of Marx as an analogy, suggesting that business
motivation in his entrepreneur economy centered on
M-C-M' (money-commodities-money) in contrast to the
"classical" economists' problem of C-M-C' (commodities-
money-commodities). As he put it, the basis of the
businessman's problem lay in unforeseen changes in
prices against which he could not provide, if his competitors followed him, by changes in production decisions or revisions in the prices embodied in contracts
with factors of production. In his substantive theory,
Keynes used two units of measurement, employment and income, with the latter defined both *ex ante*
and *ex post*, a propensity to spend or consume, a multiplier, a liquidity-preference determined rate of interest,
and a theory of the determination of investment that
began to look suspiciously like, but was not yet, the
marginal efficiency of capital. However, when he used
the theory, which still looked more like the framework
of the *Treatise* in its exact treatment of situations of
disequilibrium, the result was not altogether successful,
owing to its shifting concept of income and its still
incomplete theory of investment.

In fact, 1934 saw a swift movement toward a version
sufficiently complete for Keynes to finish the year lecturing to his Cambridge undergraduates from galley
proofs. The year's record was full of "stiff supervisions"
from Richard Kahn on fundamentals, especially the
definition of income in the model; of drafts and redrafts
that moved away from the *Treatise* framework, with
its problem of strictly defining the appropriate intervals
of time for the operational measurement of each variable, toward the comparative static framework we know
now, which fudged the problem by suppressing it; of
the development of the concept of the marginal efficiency
of capital, first as a name and later full-blown; and of

attempts, in Washington and New York (while he was in America to receive an honorary degree from Columbia University), to explain the theory in outline, with appropriate statistics, to those responsible for advice on and the execution of American policy. At the end of the year, the final series of intense discussions with fellow economists on the basis of galley proofs began in earnest.

These discussions moved in two stages. The first was a relatively barren series of exchanges with Dennis Robertson, who for various reasons, including piety to his predecessors, was not sympathetic to the work as a whole. The second, which followed further drafting sessions with Kahn, involved R. G. Hawtrey, Roy Harrod, Joan Robinson, and, of course, Kahn himself.[15] The correspondence with Hawtrey, which continued after publication, was voluminous but had little effect on the final result. The remainder, particularly that with Harrod, who, following Robertson, unsuccessfully tried to water down Keynes's violent attack on his classical predecessors, was more fruitful, leaving its marks on the detailed formulation of the final product, which appeared in English bookshops in February 1936.

It was natural that the book should be widely reviewed in both popular and technical publications. The reviews themselves were mixed, varying from considerable enthusiasm to outright hostility, with an admixture of praise and confusion in between. Naturally, enthusiastic reviews came from sympathizers who had been in on the message before publication—Abba Lerner, Brian Reddaway, David Champernowne, Roy Harrod—although Harrod, perhaps not surprisingly in the light of his comments on the proofs, went out of his way to emphasize the unrevolutionary implications of the book

[15] For the surviving elements of these discussions as enshrined in correspondence, together with the relevant drafts of the book, see *JMK*, XIII and XIV.

for economic theory. Pigou, who had acted as Keynes's "straw man" at several points in the book, reviewed it unfavorably, less for this reason than for Keynes's carping at Marshall. Others of the older generation, deeply entrenched in traditional theory, also saw little that was original in the book and reviewed it accordingly. Keynes was, however, upset that H. D. Henderson and Robertson were unable to come with him on the main issues, and he went to considerable lengths, without success, to persuade Robertson that the differences between them were very small.

Between the two extremes were a number of what might be called "mixed" reviews and commentaries, of which those by J. R. Hicks, A. H. Hansen, and Jacob Viner were perhaps the most interesting and important. Hansen's two reviews are best taken first. Although Hansen was to become the leading American expositor of Keynesian economics within a few years, his initial comments were lukewarm and dismissive, going so far as to write off the theoretical analysis completely. The discussions by Viner and Hicks are of greater interest, as they were the subjects of comment by Keynes and had important effects on the subsequent literature. Hicks's theoretical milieu at the London School of Economics[16] had been the Austrian general-equilibrium tradition which had produced actively noninterventionist policy conclusions in the face of the Depression; Viner's was at the University of Chicago, where economists working in the classical tradition had reached Keynes's policy conclusions through common-sense observation while continuing to hold to traditional theory. Both tended to play down the path-breaking aspects of the book, in particular the role of uncertainty, and attempted

[16] Hicks had only recently come to Cambridge as a university lecturer in economics.

to show that Keynes's claims rested on rather minor adjustments to the body of traditional theory which might be important for policy purposes, although Hicks was broadly much more sympathetic to the whole exercise than Viner. In replying to the two, Keynes concentrated on their treatment of uncertainty and expectations and the related question of his monetary theory of the determination of the rate of interest, the point where the existence of uncertainty made the sharpest apparent break with existing doctrine. As he put it in his reply to Viner, "Why should anyone outside a lunatic asylum wish to use money as a store of wealth?" He then went on to provide a basis for an answer: "Because, partly on reasonable and partly on instinctive grounds, our desire to hold money as a store of wealth is a barometer of the degree of our distrust of our own calculations and conventions concerning the future. . . . The possession of money lulls our disquietude; and the premium which we require to make us part with money is the measure of the degree of our disquietude" (*JMK*, XIV, 115–16).[17] It is this aspect of Keynes's contribution that is still the subject of fruitful work at the very foundations of economic theory.

In fact, the *General Theory* fell among the economists of the day with a very big bang. Nothing for any of them was ever quite the same again. The publications of working economists over the next few years attest to the book's impact. There were numerous attempts to develop a format for presenting the essentials of the theory to others, to sort out the exact meaning or implications of Keynes's building blocks, to estimate the empirical magnitudes involved, and to use Keynes's approach to understand contemporary or past problems. One preliminary

[17] For a more detailed discussion of Hicks's commentary see the Appendix, which begins on p. 171.

attempt at a bibliography ten years later uncovered some 300 articles in major professional journals commenting on Keynes's work or largely inspired by it, not to mention numerous books and monographs. Moreover, Keynes's contribution "with its happy combination of intellectual excitement and promise of social improvement"[18] drew a large part of a whole generation to economics as a serious subject. No, things were never exactly the same again—even opponents of Keynes's vision reformulated their objections within something that looked like his framework.

During the year following the publication of the *General Theory*, as well as clarifying his views for and replying to critics, encouraging the work of a younger generation of colleagues, and taking a vigorous interest in the Arts Theatre in Cambridge, which he had opened the night before the publication of the book, Keynes kept fingers in many pies. He engaged in an acrimonious correspondence over British foreign policy in the columns of the *New Statesman*, contributed an important broadcast on "Art and the State" to a BBC series, wrote an elaborate centenary memoir of W. S. Jevons for the Royal Statistical Society (*JMK*, IX), and gave a lecture to the Eugenics Society on "Some Economic Consequences of a Declining Population" (*JMK*, XIV), which looked through the glasses of the *General Theory* at the longer-run problems associated with the phenomenon—all this plus his normal pursuits.

Moreover, Keynes had started to move away from the position of the *General Theory*. The only signs of the movement that survive are pieces of lectures from the spring of 1937 from a series entitled "Footnotes to *The*

---

[18] J. Tobin, *The New Economics One Decade Older* (Princeton, 1974), p. 57.

General Theory of Employment, Interest and Money," a draft table of contents for a book of that title, and a few asides to his friends suggesting that he was now standing somewhat back from his previous work. What would have come of such a rethinking, one cannot tell, for many of his previous books had evolved from an initial series of footnotes to the book last published.[19] However, during the summer term of 1937, after feeling somewhat under the weather for some months, Keynes suffered a heart attack. Although he was eventually able to return to a substantial level of activity by his previous standards—rather phenomenal activity by the standards of others—he was never again to devote much time to economic theory. The last nine years of his life were devoted to applications of economic analysis to the problems of preparation for war, the war itself, and reconstruction.

Just prior to his heart attack, there was an indication of how quickly Keynes's views had spread into official quarters—largely because of his previous efforts at rational persuasion. During 1934, 1935, and much of 1936, the members of the Committee on Economic Information (including Keynes) and some Treasury officials had been generally satisfied with the progress of Britain's recovery from the depths of the 1929–32 slump. That recovery, based on cheap money and facilitated by the absence of direct international complications owing to a managed exchange rate, had initially taken the form of a spurt in housebuilding and then spread to other forms of investment. As it continued, observers began to worry about what would happen when housebuilding ceased to provide a stimulus for demand. Then, having made up for a previous long period of

---

[19] *A Revision of the Treaty, A Treatise on Money*, and the *General Theory* are three examples.

neglect in housing, Britain would have to depend on other stimuli to investment than such housebuilding as might occur in response to the slow growth in or movements of population, at a time when all necessary post-slump restocking of working capital and machinery had occurred. As 1936 progressed, there were signs of a raw-materials boom and an expansion of rearmament expenditure on the horizon. Late in 1936, Keynes began to prepare a series of articles of economic management, eventually published in January 1937, entitled "How to Avoid a Slump." He also made similar suggestions to the Committee on Economic Information, which adopted them in its February 1937 report, despite Robertson's objections to Keynes's views on monetary policy. Robertson, however, agreed on the public-works proposals.

In his *Times* articles Keynes concentrated on the avoidance of future fluctuations in demand. Given future prospects, he suggested, the major task of economic policy was to prevent a situation where the existing boom overreached itself, disappointed expectations, and led to a reduction in investment He also suggested that the authorities should keep available replacements in the form of nonrecurrent types of investment for use once the recovery had exhausted available opportunities, so that they could then step in to sustain demand. Arguing that the recovery had reached a point where general stimuli to demand were becoming redundant, he suggested that the authorities should devote more effort on behalf of the depressed areas which had shared incompletely in the recovery thus far—aiming for the right distribution of demand rather than its general expansion.

Keynes then turned to other means of sustaining the recovery and preventing its collapse, in particular the use of interest-rate policy to restrain investment expenditure. Although, in the past, dearer money had accompanied booms, especially toward the end, he argued that the authorities should avoid dearer money as they would hell-fire; for, once they made money dearer, they would find it hard to reverse the upward trend in interest rates. He continued: "A low enough long-term rate of interest cannot be achieved if we allow it to be believed that better terms will be obtainable from time to time by those who keep their resources liquid. The long-term rate of interest must be kept *continuously* as near as possible to what we believe to be the long-term optimum. It is not suitable to be used as a short-period weapon." As a result, given his expectation that deficient demand would be the longer-term problem facing the British economy, he urged the authorities to use taxation policy, especially in financing rearmament, tariff reductions, and the careful planning of public works to restrain and, therefore, stretch out the boom.[20]

Much of his advice might have been expected of the author of the *General Theory*, knowing his longer-term expectations.[21] What was unusual in the circumstances was the reaction of the authorities. By the mid-1930s they had abandoned most of their earlier theoretical objections to public works—to the way they diverted

---

[20] He saw some minor role for monetary policy in that moral suasion might, through raising margin requirements, reduce the scope for stock-exchange speculation and hence keep any business expectations based on share prices steadier.

[21] Lord Kahn has recently suggested that Keynes, by advising restraint at a time when unemployment exceeded one million, wished to maintain "a considerable reserve army of unemployed" to meet the needs of the re-armament programme he desired and recognised as inevitable ("What Keynes Really Said," *The Sunday Telegraph,* September 24, 1974). While such a construction on Keynes's advice may be possible, I have not as yet come across sufficient evidence to support it.

resources from the private sector or affected the possibilities of funding the national debt—in favor of the argument that public works took so long to put into operation that they would not be useful over a short period or the argument that public works were unnecessary, given cheap money and protection—a line of argument strongly favored by Neville Chamberlain as Chancellor. By the end of 1936, however, Sir Frederick Phillips had come around to views somewhat closer to Keynes's. For several years, Phillips had been an interested observer of the ongoing monetary debates and had been less inclined to treat them as irrelevant to the practical problems, for which he was responsible, than most of his colleagues. Having independently reached the same broad policy conclusions as Keynes and the Committee on Economic Information, he used its views to try, with some success, to persuade ministers to act on the recommendations on public works, taxation policy, and trade policy.

The steps which followed included full interdepartmental consideration of the recommendations, a process which took some time, owing to the frequent absence abroad of the government's chief economic adviser. By the time definite recommendations favoring the postponement of appropriate public-works schemes were ready for the cabinet, it was August 1937 and the long-awaited recession had arrived. Interestingly enough, though, the relevant committee then turned to revising its recommendations and advocated the setting in hand of additional public-works schemes as well as the forward planning of future schemes to aid countercyclical policy. Thus, in a limited way, the influence of the Keynesian revolution reached Whitehall very soon after the publication of the *General Theory*. As far as one can tell, the same influence reached Washington soon afterward in plans devised to meet the same recession. True, the acceptance of the ideas was far from complete, as contemporary British official discussions of budgetary policies and monetary policies surrounding rearmament indicate. But it represented a beginning. World War II was to make a considerable difference.

The Economist Statesman, 1939–46

VI

Between his heart attack in 1937 and the outbreak of war, Keynes was more or less out of action. True, he continued to edit the *Economic Journal*, contribute to discussions of policy through *The Times* and the Committee on Economic Information, play a useful role in his college, and contribute occasional articles of review or comment to professional journals. His energies were so much directed to achieving, with the collaboration of many minds, an acceptance of something similar to his views in the *General Theory*, or in discussing the problems of preparing for a possible war, that it is possible to deal with his work during this period either in passing, as in the previous chapter, or in the context of his wartime activities.

World War II, like World War I, saw Keynes deeply involved in the formulation of economic policy, at first as a well-connected outsider, later as an unofficial and often rather irregular insider. But Keynes's role differed considerably from what it had been in 1915–19. In 1939 he was by far the most distinguished British economist of his generation, both in the eyes of "the profession" and among the wider public. This public stature, together with the connections forged over previous years, gave Keynes much greater and easier access to, and opportunities to influence, official and unofficial opinion. On the other hand, during the war, he held no official position beyond his membership of the Chancellor of the Exchequer's Consultative Council, set up in the summer of 1940— which this did not of itself entitle him to a room in the Treasury. In fact, he was cheaper than the American dollar-a-year man, for he received nothing for his services beyond his expenses on official missions abroad.

These differences from the 1915–19 arrangements meant that the forms of his involvement differed considerably from those of the earlier period: "he was just 'Keynes,' free to shoot at anybody—and anybody, regardless of rank, was free to go to him with his troubles" as Dennis Proctor, a Kingsman Treasury official, put it. Being "just 'Keynes'" had its advantages, of course; for it meant that he could, and did, take these troubles further—to where they mattered. Thus, a matter might come to his attention from members of the Treasury, from friends and colleagues (both economist and non-economist) in other departments, from friends outside Whitehall, or from his own voracious (but often selective) reading of official papers from all sources. The result might be a volley of minutes (frequently supported by forthcoming or recently published articles from the *Economic Journal* or press clippings) aimed at several in-trays, or word with a friend in a high place that would lead to further inquiries from a higher level (which Keynes might then be asked to reply to), or a personal letter. One official summarized Keynes's working habits and their irregularity in a letter to a colleague at the time of the setting up of the Arts Council as follows: "Keynes pushes the Minister: the Minister pushes Wood, and Wood is, therefore, constrained to write this letter to you. In short, both Keynes and the Minister ask why. . . ."[1]

As a "demi-semi-official" (Keynes's own term for his status), he was free to get other departments or politicians to agree on emerging policies at a much earlier stage than normal. As "Keynes" he found himself regularly consulted by and consulting J. G. Winant, the American Ambassador, and his adviser E. F. Penrose; visiting American officials, such as Oscar Cox and Harry Hopkins, journalists such as Walter Lippmann (many of whose letters on American conditions and opinion went via Keynes to senior officials and ministers); and foreign officials and ambassadors such as I. M. Maisky, the Russian Ambassador. As "Keynes" he could, and did, consult the General Council of the Trades Union Congress at a meeting called to discuss his war-finance proposals, as well as other leaders of opinion. The upshot was that, very much more than in the 1930s, Keynes was a "political" economist, whose influence, although it never equaled the brilliance of his pen, was unique in the annals of modern economic policy.

If only because the range of subjects that interested him in the six years of war and eight months of peace before his death is vast, I must, of necessity, be selective.[2] All I can do is give something of the flavor of the

---

[1] Letter from Sir Robert Wood (Board of Education) to Sir Alan Barlow (Treasury), February 14, 1945. The minister in question was R. A. Butler.

[2] In addition to the more well-known matters of wartime finance and postwar planning touched on below, Keynes's

principles and practice of the wartime Keynes at work and relate his major wartime concerns, where possible, to earlier ideas. To do this, I shall look at his activities in four areas: internal wartime finance, internal postwar economic policy planning, external wartime finance, and external postwar economic policy.

Wartime financial policy is concerned with a rather limited range of general principles, although their application can be very complex in particular cases. Any policy proposal must satisfy, in various ways, four criteria: it must intensify the nation's war effort by mobilizing domestic resources for war and maintaining that mobilization; it must increase the resources available by drawing, as far as possible, on unused resources at home and resources from abroad; it must make the burdens resulting from these transfers of resources from their normal peacetime uses as tolerable as possible; and it must minimize the complications of the war that spill over into the postwar world. All these criteria involve both action and persuasion, for in a democracy at war what is possible within given limits, and even the limits themselves, depend on what is tolerable—on what public opinion in its inner and outer forms believes just. From the outset—even from before the outset—Keynes involved himself in the problems of war finance on two fronts: maximizing the possible under the existing constraints, and easing the constraints themselves.

Keynes's contributions to discussions of the problems

interests and influence extended to such matters as the postwar rebuilding of London, colonial development policy, the preservation of art treasures in Italy, war aims, export finance, the postwar cotton trade, postwar labor-management relations, nationalization, and, of course, the forerunner of the Arts Council, the Committee for the Encouragement of Music and the Arts (CEMA).

of internal wartime finance began, despite his illness, well before the outbreak of war. For more than two years he had discussed the economics of *preparing* for war— the economics in Britain of the 1930s of the movement toward full employment—in memoranda to ministers and officials, articles, broadcasts, and letters to the press. In these discussions, largely concentrated on monetary policy, Keynes emphasized the following points:

1. The authorities should avoid higher interest rates. The long-term rate of interest for wartime borrowing should not exceed 2.5 per cent (the rate which Keynes had advocated as a goal for several years). Such a rate would provide continuity with previous peacetime rates, not disturb the psychological factors at the basis of market behavior, and, once the difficulties had passed, leave the authorities' hands free to move to lower rates after the war.

2. To obtain the necessary real resources for rearmament, the authorities should rely on taxation and, as output approached full employment, physical and financial controls.

3. Having fixed their interest-rate policy under (1) and maintained Bank rate at the 1930s level of 2 per cent, the authorities should allow the public to hold the maturity structure of the public debt it preferred, and make a wide enough range of securities available to allow it to exercise a choice.

4. When they did borrow (especially before the outbreak of war, when resources were less than fully employed), the authorities should do so *after* incurring the expenditure, when the savings resulting from an associated rise in income via the multiplier became available for placement in financial markets. This policy would avoid transitional pressures on these markets and thus help to preserve the desired structure of interest rates.

This implied an initial period of credit expansion to "finance" the rise in expenditure in its early stages.[3]

The outbreak of war, which Keynes, assuming a repetition of Munich, appears not to have foreseen as late as August 25, 1939, brought the prospect of full mobilization *and* full employment, obviously a different situation. Keynes responded quickly with the bundle of ideas subsequently associated with *How to Pay for the War*, published in February 1940 (*JMK*, IX). As the story of how the message was evolved and what tactics were used of its presentation provide a classic example of Keynes as a practical political economist at work, it is worth looking at these matters in more detail.

Keynes first broached the message of *How to Pay for the War* in a talk on October 20, 1939, to the Marshall Society (the undergraduate society in the Faculty of Economics at Cambridge) entitled "War Potential and War Finance." Four days later, he sent a draft of his proposals, now entitled "The Limitation of Purchasing Power: High Prices, Taxation and Compulsory Savings," to the editor of *The Times*, Sir John Simon (the Chancellor of the Exchequer), Clement Attlee (the Leader of the Opposition), R. H. Brand, and Sir Josiah Stamp, H. D. Henderson, and Henry Clay of the Government's Survey of Economic and Financial Plans.[4] On October 27 he spoke to a dinner meeting of officials, ministers, and M.P.s, later circulating copies of his draft proposals

[3] The formalization of this idea of finance, although in some ways a throwback to ideas of the *Treatise*, resulted from the post-*General Theory* controversy with Dennis Robertson and others (see *JMK*, XIV, 207–10, 218–20, 229–33).

[4] The Stamp Survey, as it was known, had grown out of the Committee on Economic Information just before the outbreak of war. It eventually evolved into the Economic Section of the War Cabinet and the Central Statistical Office.

to those interested. As a result of the ensuing discussions and comments, he modified them—dropping, for example, a suggested guarantee of the real value of the compulsory savings because he thought it might deflect subsequent discussion from his more important substantive proposals—before they appeared in *The Times* on November 14 and 15, 1939, under the title of "Paying for the War."[5] Between the publication of the articles and the appearance of the pamphlet *How to Pay for the War*, Keynes entered into extensive discussions, both in private and in the newspapers (including papers more "popular" than *The Times*), to get across the reasoning behind his scheme and to find ways of making it more generally acceptable. In particular, he directly (and indirectly through Professor Harold Laski, G. D. H. Cole, and Kingsley Martin) attempted to convince the Labour party and trade-union leaders (who had been, to put it mildly, unenthusiastic about his original proposals) of the soundness of his underlying principles while altering details to make the scheme more acceptable to them. On January 24, for example, he spent the morning with members of the Labour front bench before going on in the afternoon to a committee of the General Council of the TUC.

In the weeks that followed, he spoke to meetings of members of the House of Commons, the Fabian Society, and the National Trade Union Club, while continuing his discussions with fellow economists of all political persuasions, City representatives, and friends. As a result of this process of discussion, he introduced several modifications into the original scheme for deferred pay on compulsory savings: family allowances to protect the

---

[5] Owing to a leak through a neutral correspondent at proof stage, the articles first appeared in the German press.

low paid with large families, stabilization of the prices of the basic articles of consumption covered in the cost-of-living index, and a postwar capital levy to repay the compulsory savings and redistribute wealth.

· After publication, which coincided with a debate in the House of Lords that he had arranged through a sympathetic peer, and a broadcast on March 11, **Keynes** continued to press for the adoption of his policy, both privately and publicly. However, his continued lack of real success, especially with the politicians, brought a change in tactics. As he told Clement Davies, a sympathetic MP, on May 3:

> There is not the slightest hope of getting any useful attention at this stage. Things have clearly got to stew for a bit yet. . . . I feel one must wait until the progress of events is making some new action obviously necessary.
>
> At the present stage I believe there is a good deal to be said for concentrating on the inadequacy of the spending programme rather than the inadequacy of the fiscal programme. If we can get what is wanted in the former respect, the inadequacy of the latter will soon be shown up.

Keynes thus proceeded to concentrate on the inadequacies of the expenditure program.

The German campaign in the west and the fall of France in June 1940 provided the necessary stimulus to government expenditure. They also brought about a political crisis: the fall of Neville Chamberlain and the Cabinet changes which took Keynes into the Treasury as a member of the Consultative Council of the new Chancellor, Sir Kingsley Wood, and as his unofficial adviser. Once within the Whitehall machine, with new ministers and the climate prepared by the turn of events and his own previous exercises in persuasion, Keynes was extremely successful in gaining acceptance of his principles and methods of analysis, if not the exact details of his proposals. The 1941 budget, which set the pattern for all subsequent wartime financial policy, was truly Keynesian in inspiration and presentation.

So much for the background, which shows Keynes the "political" economist in his prime. What of the principles involved? Throughout the discussions after the outbreak of war, Keynes's main concern was with the best method of transferring resources from peacetime to wartime uses, especially from consumption.[6] Before the war, this had not been a problem, as the authorities had been able to draw on previously unused resources to meet both the needs of rearmament and the multiplier repercussions of increased government expenditure. Keynes's main concern then had been to ensure that the financial market implications of the expansion of demand and its financing did not upset the long-term policy of cheap money which he believed necessary for the economy. War, however, made the problem of trans-

[6] Keynes also allowed for decreases in investment and sales of overseas assets or increases in overseas liabilities (on which see pp. 138–39). To give some indication of what happened, a comparison of 1938 and the peak war-effort year of 1944 is instructive. Taking the national accounts for the two years (plus the intervening years' declines in stockbuilding) the figures look as follows: increased output (largely achieved by 1940–41) £1320 million, decreased consumers' expenditures £530 million, decreased investment £220 million, deterioration on current account £140 million. The figures, at 1938 constant prices, are from C. H. Feinstein, *National Income, Expenditure and Output of the United Kingdom, 1855–1965*, (Cambridge, 1972), Appendix Table 5. The figures exclude the depreciation on wear and tear not made good during the period. This was certainly substantial after 1940.

ferring resources acute, for not only would the war effort take up any possible further increases in output but it would also require real resources normally devoted to other uses, particularly consumption. From Keynes's point of view, the authorities could gain command of the additional resources (apart from any decline in investment, living on past stocks, or deterioration in the current account) in four ways:

1. Individuals could voluntarily reduce their consumption expenditure and directly or indirectly make their savings available to the authorities by taking up loans or increasing their idle balances.

2. Inflationary official policies could initially bid the necessary resources away from those who might use them and place them in the hands of those who would pass them on eventually to the authorities through taxation or voluntary savings.

3. A policy of comprehensive rationing could reduce consumption by fiat.

4. Increased taxation could reduce the resources available to the public for consumption and transfer them to the authorities.

Given the magnitude of the sums involved and the consequent need for a sharp rise in the average (and marginal) propensity to save, especially among groups that had not previously saved much, Keynes believed that voluntary savings would not provide the resources necessary for the successful prosecution of the war without resorting to inflation. Although inflation might, up to a point, prove effective in reducing consumption, after this point further price rises would lead, with a lag, to offsetting wage claims. Given the likely lags, prosecution of the war by this method of finance would necessitate large and *continuous* price increases, with their associated discontent, inequities, and charges of profiteering

(*JMK*, IX, 413–25).[7] As for rationing *by itself* as a means of restricting consumption, Keynes believed (wrongly, as it turned out) that it would prove much too restrictive of personal choice and therefore give rise to dissatisfaction; that it would prove socially divisive, as those with higher incomes could get around any less than comprehensive scheme; and that the complexities of a comprehensive scheme (in the days before the notion of points rationing as a replacement for fixed-quantity rationing had become prevalent) would be too great an administrative burden when the object of any measure was to release the maximum volume of resources for wartime purposes.

Thus, by elimination, fiscal measures found themselves at the center of Keynes's wartime financial vision. Through taxation, the authorities would take command over current resources from present income earners for wartime purposes. A portion of such command over resources, credited to the taxpayer as postwar deferred pay, would be released to expand consumption in the first postwar slump. The "forced savings" arising from the deferred-pay scheme and the release of the sums involved through a postwar capital levy would insure a much more equitable postwar distribution of wealth than would the voluntary savings or inflationary methods of finance. At the same time, a subsidy scheme for the basic articles of consumption, themselves largely subject

[7] Keynes believed that workers would accept a fall of up to 10 per cent in their standard of living before pressing for higher money wages. After that point, wages would follow prices with a lag largely determined by the institutional conditions surrounding wage-bargaining. In the 1914–18 war, the lag had been about six months to a year, but in the conditions of 1939–40, with the trade unions more index conscious, the lag would be shorter and, hence, the price rises necessary for the given transfer of resources larger than they had been in 1914–18, when the cost of living had risen by 125 per cent.

to rationing, would stabilize demand on working-class family budgets, and, along with family allowances, provide for a strong element of social justice during the war. This set of arrangements—with the assistance of rationing, heavy taxation of inessential consumption, and voluntary savings—would provide the resources from personal consumption to wage total war successfully, while physical and financial controls would restrict unnecessary wartime investment and other controls would manage the external position.

Keynes's proposals, as we have noted, lay at the heart of the financial policy eventually adopted,[8] as did his method of analyzing the extent of the problem and the appropriateness of particular measures in an explicit *General Theory* macroeconomic accounting framework rather than the narrow Treasury framework which looked only at the government accounts. After the 1941 Budget Statement, the first British Budget Statement cast in this broader economic framework, Keynes spent the rest of the war attempting to improve on the details of his fiscal vision, not always with success, until the prospects of peace turned him toward proposals designed to ease the eventual transition. It is significant that on the day of his death he was engaged in writing yet another memorandum on budgetary policy, one designed to continue the transition to more normal conditions. The Keynesian approach to the problems of budgetary policy represents one of his most enduring contributions to the conduct of public affairs.

One implication of the taxation and exchange-control policies adopted by the authorities after 1939 was that the rate of interest was not expected to play either of

[8] Here I speak only of financial policy. The successful prosecution of the war depended on much more than financial measures which partly served to supplement physical controls and manpower allocations.

its 1914–18 functions of transferring real resources to the authorities from residents or from foreigners holding short-term sterling balances. As we have seen, throughout the 1930s, through slump and rearmament, Keynes had encouraged a policy of low long-term rates and attacked the rise in rates that post-1932 funding and official passivity had engendered. His persuasion had been influential, for it created a climate of opinion which made war and cheap money seem compatible to the authorities even before he entered the Treasury. However, Keynes's arrival, after market expectations of continuing cheap money had been disturbed by the brief, inexplicable, doubling of Bank rate to 4 per cent at the outbreak of war and the relative failure of the first large war loan, toughened the Treasury's nerve as regards cheap money and encouraged it to groom the market for better terms from a Treasury point of view with each successive issue, thus keeping up the demand for debt in the short-term and encouraging expectations of lower long-term interest rates after the war. In addition, Keynes's understanding of the determinants of the term structure of interest rates (something the Treasury had lacked throughout the 1930s) encouraged the authorities to tailor the available issues to market preferences so as to ensure a structure of rates consistent with their long-term policy goals. This concern was to carry itself over into Keynes's proposals for the postwar period, as was his view of the role of financial controls.

Throughout his discussions of internal wartime financial policy, Keynes kept his eye firmly fixed on the postwar situation. He also influenced the development of postwar internal economic policy in Britain, most particularly in three directions: the method of analysis used in assessing the aggregate impact of various postwar policies; the 1944 White Paper on Employment Policy; and the 1945 National Debt Enquiry.

After he had successfully introduced the mode of thought into the budget discussions of 1940–41, Keynes's macroeconomic approach to many economic problems came to be used in other areas of policy formulation. Initially, following their experience in estimating wartime potential output, those using his framework tended to work from the supply side only, but, under Keynes's increasing optimism as to the level of demand during the transition, they turned to consider both sides of the relationship in estimating the postwar national income. Such estimates of postwar incomes and activity came to be used extensively in inquiries like the Treasury and Economic Section evaluation of the Beveridge social-insurance proposals prior to its publication, for they provided the authorities with a crude but improved view as to what the nation could "afford" in the postwar world, given other claims upon resources. One result of the Beveridge exercise was a series of representations to Beveridge by Keynes, Robbins, and the Government Actuary which led to a marked trimming of the scope of the original proposals in the drafting stage.

The most frequent use of Keynesian modes of analysis came in discussions of postwar policy. From *How to Pay for the War* onwards, Keynes was convinced of the need to avoid, as far as possible in an open economy, a repetition of Britain's interwar experience of high unemployment. The permanent Treasury officials, however, perhaps partly because of the interwar record and partly as a result of the absence of Sir Frederick Phillips (the most "Keynesian" of the senior officials who was in America for most of the time after 1940), were generally pessimistic as to the postwar prospect, the most optimistic of them doubting the ability of economic management to do more than regain "the pre-war optimum of 10%" unemployment. One senior official, at one stage, even went to the length of asking James Meade of the Economic Section about the section's attitude toward a deliberate policy of postwar deflation.

Keynes's own views as to economic prospects changed over time. In 1929 he was advocating expansion when unemployment stood at one million; in 1937 he had become much more pessimistic as to the prospects of the economy, and consequently advocated measures to restrain the boom when unemployment was well above that figure. In *How to Pay for the War* this pessimism remained, and he appears to have believed that a slump would follow soon after the end of the war. Hence his suggestion for the repayment of deferred pay in such circumstances and the emphasis he gave it and the associated capital levy, suggested by F. A. Hayek, in the pamphlet. By 1943 he had come to expect that high levels of demand would be the norm for ten to fifteen years after the war, and he was coming to regard unemployment as high as 800,000 as a very pessimistic assumption for postwar forecasts of national income. When his colleagues, estimating the level of income from the supply side, tended to assume levels as high as 1.2 to 1.5 million in their forecasts, Keynes was moved to protest strongly that demand conditions after the war would make such forecasts nonsensical.

In these circumstances, it is perhaps not surprising that Keynes did not push on his own for a more active approach to the problems of postwar employment. Given his other extremely time-consuming wartime preoccupations, he apparently believed that such an effort, at the expense of work elsewhere, was unnecessary. This belief seems to have rested as well on three other premises: a successful postwar employment policy, unlike, say, social-security policy, required little in the way of concrete planning and even less in the way of actual wartime legislation; its success would depend heavily on

Britain's external economic position, increasingly the center of Keynes's concern; and the ingredients necessary to it were under consideration in various reconstruction committees, even if they were not specifically directed to the employment problem. Most important was his belief that unemployment would not be a problem for several years after the war.

A consequence of Keynes's fairly minor involvement was that the early Treasury documents for the Committee on Post-War Internal Economic Problems (the body set up initially to consider postwar employment prospects) were the work of Hubert Henderson. He had been unsympathetic to the Keynes-inspired changes in economic theory during the 1930s and was one of the Treasury's leading pessimists as to the possibility of providing any solution to the problem of unemployment in the postwar world. It was the Economic Section, in particular James Meade, which provided the drive for an activist solution from 1941 onward. Granted that Keynes used his considerable influence to ease the passage of certain proposals, in particular Meade's countercyclical variations in social insurance contributions, which he pushed to inclusion in the Beveridge Report, the 1944 White Paper on Employment Policy, and the 1944 White Paper on Social Insurance. However, within the Treasury, he appears to have felt that he need do no more than prevent major Treasury blunders while officials drafted meliorative replies, one of which Keynes characterized as "not much more than Neville Chamberlain disguised in a little modern fancy dress," to successive activist Economic Section papers for official committees. At the same time, he informally prevented the section's documents from becoming too "academic." When the Steering Committee on Post-War Employment reported early in 1944, he welcomed the document as "a revolution in official opinion," despite its Treasury sections with their "air of having been written some years before the rest of the report." Proclaiming that "theoretical economics has now reached a point where it is fit to be applied," he foresaw "a new era of 'Joy through Statistics'" as the policy came into operation.

After this welcome, Keynes's drafting contributions to the White Paper which followed were few, because of his involvement in an extensive official and ministerial debate on postwar external economic policy and his illness during March and April 1944, the months of heaviest drafting. However, in addition to the comment to T. S. Eliot quoted above (p. 35), another remark to Sir William Beveridge at the end of 1944 seems to indicate the point his own thinking had reached: "No harm in aiming at 3 per cent unemployment, but I shall be surprised if we succeed"—his pessimism being due to his awareness that the British economy was vulnerable to depressive influences from abroad.

As for the preferred method of achieving full employment, Keynes consistently maintained his view of the 1930s that it was desirable to concentrate on the stimulation of investment. As he put it to Josiah Wedgwood (a fellow director of the Bank of England) in July 1943:

The question then arises why I should prefer rather a heavy scale of investment to increasing consumption. My main reason for this is that I do not think we have yet reached anything like the point of capital saturation. It would be in the interest of the standard of life in the long run if we increased our capital quite materially. After twenty years of large-scale investment I should expect to have to change my mind. Even in the meanwhile it is a question of degree. But certainly for the first ten years after the war—and I should expect another ten years after that—it would not be in the interests of the community to encourage more expenditure on food and drink at the expense of expenditure on housing. For that broadly is what it would come to.

There is also a subsidiary point that, at the present stage of things, it is very much easier socially and politically to influence the rate of investment than to influence the rate of consumption. No doubt you can encourage consumption by giving things away right and left. But that will mean that you will have to collect by taxation, what people would otherwise save and devote to investment,—all of which would be a stiff job in the existing political and social set-up. Perhaps you may say that that is a reason for getting rid of the existing political and social set-up. But is it clear that expenditure on housing and public utilities is so obviously injurious that one ought to attempt a social revolution in order to get rid of it?

This philosopher-king assumption of knowing what was best for the public and encouraging accumulation first so as to reach the point where further accumulation, with its concomitant requirement of an unequal distribution of income, was unnecessary, had long been a part of Keynes's vision. Once the economic problem of accumulation to achieve an adequate standard of living for all had receded, then men could turn from the economic problem, to "value ends above means and prefer the good to the useful." Then would come the social revolution. Then free enterprise might safely go by the boards.

Characteristically, Keynes's most substantial direct contribution to discussions of postwar employment policy concerned investment stimulation along more traditional Keynesian lines, that of monetary policy. A request from Clement Attlee, the Deputy Prime Minister, for a memorandum for guidance on a postwar capital levy provided the excuse for the organization of a National Debt Enquiry Committee with wide terms of reference allowing it to range over monetary policy, debt-management policy, a capital levy, and changes in the format of the budget to aid management for full employment. Besides Keynes, two other professional economists were members, James Meade and Lionel Robbins.

The committee actually spent little time on a capital levy, or "capital levity" as Keynes called it, given the evolution of his views as to postwar prospects since 1940. The early stages saw monetary and debt-management policy issues at the fore. Keynes dominated these, giving "private evidence" for three meetings, in which he offered an exposition of how he approached the theory of savings and investment, the determination of the rate of interest, and the consequences of changes in the structure of interest rates, before coming to recommend a specific monetary policy for Britain during the transition. The assumptions underlying his recommendation were as follows:

1. After the transitional period, which, as we have seen, Keynes expected to be lengthy, deflation rather than inflation would prove to be the more likely danger.

2. The postwar world would see exchange controls on private capital movements as the normal state of affairs. It would also, in Britain's case, see the bulk of her wartime sterling balances written off or blocked. (On this subject, see below, p. 141).

3. The transition would see the maintenance of wartime consumer rationing, controls on key materials, controls on investment, and high taxation.

4. Keynes certainly realized that full employment would produce inflationary pressures owing to the effects of the changed environment on money wage claims. As he put it, "The task of keeping efficiency-wages reasonably stable (I am sure that they will creep up steadily in spite of our best efforts) is a political rather than an

economic problem." In these circumstances, Keynes seems to have acted as he noted in a comment on the Australian Full Employment White Paper: "One is also, simply because one knows no solution, inclined to turn a blind eye to the wages problem in a full employment economy" (letters dated December 1944 and June 1945).

Given these assumptions, which relieved monetary policy of the tasks of managing short-term international capital flows and of bearing the main anti-inflationary burden, and his theoretical approach to the problems involved, which followed the lines of the *General Theory* with slight adjustments for subsequent discussions, Keynes took the view that in the short term, monetary policy should meet official and social needs while leaving the authorities the maximum freedom of action in the longer term. The short-term aim should be the maintenance of cheap money, to create appropriate expectations for the longer term, with the authorities deciding on a desirable structure of interest rates and letting the public hold the available debt in the form determined by their liquidity preferences. On no account should the Treasury attempt to fund or impose its own "counter-liquidity preference," although Keynes allowed that they could use changes in short-term rates of interest, and, more important to him, through the use of moral suasion limit the volume of bank credit available to support short-term economic management. Of course, if the prevailing long-term rate became *chronically* too low, in the sense that it encouraged long-term capital formation on an inflationary scale, long rates should rise, but he did not expect this to happen. At all stages, however, the authorities should maintain some uncertainty in the market, because certainty as to the rate of interest would monetize the whole national debt. As he put in his rough notes for his evidence: "Bridges [the enquiry's chairman] said game was up when everyone understood it. In fact the game is only up when the public believe that the Treasury understands it."

Keynes's analysis and proposals, including his recommended structure of rates, met with general agreement and a report, drafted by Sir Richard Hopkins, embodying them (and adorned with appropriate quotations from the *General Theory*, which Hopkins read for the first time during the enquiry) went to the Chancellor on May 15, 1945. The recommendations certainly can be regarded as the basis of Dr. Hugh Dalton's post-1945 experiments with cheap money, although one wonders if Keynes would have approved of the tactics employed.

So far, I have only touched in passing on external financial policy, despite the fact that it was the major claim on Keynes's energies throughout the war and up to his death and probably had more to do with the timing of his death than anything else. Again, keeping to the general principles of war finance mentioned above in mind, it is probably best to begin with a brief glance at wartime policy before proceeding to postwar planning.

Soon after the outbreak of war, Keynes, although heavily preoccupied with his grand internal financial plan and far from fit physically, actively entered discussions on external issues. He sent the Treasury a memorandum on exchange-control policy, the Ministry of Economic Warfare a memorandum on financial aspects of the blockade against Germany, and drafted, in collaboration with others, a memorandum intended for President Roosevelt, but which was never used, owing to the pressure of events, on America's financial role in the prosecution of the war. After the publication of *How to Pay for the War*, he returned to external problems, arguing that a more effective exchange-control policy was necessary to conserve Britain's overseas assets for the prosecution of the war. Thus, even before entering the Treasury Keynes had developed a set of principles to guide external financial policy, and he proceeded to apply them as particular cases arose. The principles and their application often bore the stamp of bitter experience from the 1914–18 war, for in many of his minutes and memoranda on external financial matters "last time" often came in as a justification for avoiding or undertaking certain courses of action. Briefly put, Keynes's principles were:

1. Through an effective exchange control, Britain should husband her exchange reserves and other external assets for future use in obtaining wartime resources. Careful overseas purchasing, particularly large forward purchases in countries which had lost markets as the result of the war and were in a weaker bargaining position, would assist the objective of this policy.

2. The authorities should attempt to minimize the postwar consequences of any sale of foreign assets under (1).

3. Britain should try to obtain access to the maximum volume of foreign resources from sterling area and other countries, again taking care to minimize the postwar consequences of any liabilities arising.

4. In her economic warfare against the enemy, Britain should encourage financial as against physical measures. In particular, as it was unlikely that she could prevent the enemy using its foreign assets, she should —through pre-emptive buying, price policies, and other controls—attempt to insure that the enemy authorities were "tempted" to waste their resources on inessential or very expensive products. At the same time, through similar policies, Britain should minimize the possible financial gains from enemy exports. Keynes's principle as regards the "temptation" of the enemy was rejected

at the outbreak of war. All of the other principles, however, found ready adoption. Only a few examples are possible.

By the time Keynes entered the Treasury, to some extent as a result of his agitation (through memoranda and speeches, as well as encouraging sympathetic M.P.s to ask questions in the House of Commons), most of the gaps in Britain's foreign-exchange controls had been eliminated. Those which had not were the subject of one of Keynes's first memoranda. Subsequent discussion at the Exchange Control Conference, set up to consider the memorandum and take action on it and on similar questions as they arose later, closed most of the remaining loopholes. However, the fall of France and the hope (which Keynes had shared with many officials since the outbreak of war) that the United States would recognize the necessity that she come to Britain's aid in solving the external financial problem had led to the abandonment of the principle that Britain's external assets would have to last a three-year war, if only because Britain's very survival was at stake.

Thus Keynes's first eighteen months at the Treasury, despite the passage of the Lend Lease Act in March 1941, were more often concerned with finding new sources of foreign exchange to keep Britain's war effort afloat than in the careful husbanding and conservation of the existing stock. A counterpart to the search for new sources of foreign exchange was the attempt to minimize the postwar consequences of using any British external assets to raise badly needed cash. Even before he had entered the Treasury, Keynes had attempted to persuade his friend Samuel Courtauld to use the assets of Courtaulds Ltd.'s American subsidiary, American Viscose, as security for a dollar bond issue, the proceeds of which would go to the British Treasury. Such an issue would provide the Treasury with badly needed dollars, leave Courtaulds in control of the subsidiary, and make any American attempts to force a sale of the subsidiary unattractive. Despite his failure to get a positive response from Samuel Courtauld on this occasion, Keynes continued to press for the alternative of borrowing against existing assets, particularly direct investments, as against outright sale, both before and after U.S. Treasury Secretary Henry Morgenthau's announcement of his intention to insist on the sale of such assets before Britain received Lend Lease aid. Keynes's emphasis on borrowing, which maximized the present and future value of such assets, given the importance of trade connections, patents, and other intra-firm links, was not entirely successful, as the "show" sale of American Viscose at a knockdown price indicates. However, the repeated suggestion of the borrowing alternative created a climate of opinion in London that made it possible for Keynes to try the idea on American officals in London early in 1941. These discussions, along with later talks in Washington, some of which took place in the course of Keynes's 1941 American visit, resulted in two large pledges of British assets as security for American loans. This raised over $425 million for Britain at a crucial stage of the war. Similarly, Keynes's repeated emphasis on the undesirability of Britain's being stripped of all her foreign assets and thus being completely open to American pressures as to the shape of her overseas commitments, along with the views of other Treasury advisers and officials, helped to prevent the panic sale of many sterling-dominated overseas assets in the dark days of the autumn of 1940, when Britain was perpetually "scraping the bottom of the box" while carrying on the war alone.

Keynes's continuous concern with the postwar consequences of wartime acts and agreements permeated his advice on other aspects of wartime external finance. It saw him successfully urge the refusal of a large dollar loan to Newfoundland and urge her postwar union with Canada; negotiate, so he thought at the time, arrangements with the United States for Stage II of Lend Lease (the period between the defeat of Germany and that of Japan) which allowed Britain to begin to use her available foreign resources to maximize her export potential for the difficult postwar transition, while relying on American aid for other more specifically military purposes; and try, without much success, to temper Britain's potential postwar overseas commitments to her prospective international economic position.

Inevitably, Keynes's concern over Britain's postwar international economic position led him into discussions of the problems raised by her growing sterling indebtedness to the rest of the world. His first efforts took the form of trying to prevent accumulations of sterling by China and Greece, both of whom asked for sterling backing for the wartime rise in the domestic note issue. However, despite their initial lack of concern with the position in sterling-area countries (in particular India and Egypt) and official worries as late as January 1942 that these countries might end the war with insufficient balances to finance normal trade, Keynes turned his Treasury colleagues' minds toward the problem with a long series of proposals designed to reduce the rate of growth of such balances or so to immobilize those that did develop that they would not provide a treat to Britain's postwar external position.

Except for a proposal to sell gold and silver at premium prices on Middle Eastern bazaar markets, so as to attract idle balances previously hoarded in commodities (thus reducing inflationary pressures and restoring confidence in local currencies while financing Allied local currency expenditures at little cost to the reserves and without the accumulation of sterling balances), most of the proposals for dealing with the developing situation arose from repeated discussions of the Indian problem. There, the special character of the wartime defense arrangements, together with inflation and changed trade patterns, resulted in large Indian accumulations of sterling. The complications presented by the political developments surrounding Britain and India's fitful movement toward the 1947 solution of independence prevented much, if anything, in the way of a solution while the war lasted.

As a result, Keynes and his colleagues, after several fruitless wartime attempts to tackle the problem, left it for the postwar clearup. During the discussions preceding Britain's approach to the United States for financial assistance for the transition from war to peace, Keynes received ministerial approval for a proposal that the Indian and other balances (which by the end of the war exceeded £2500 million) be released, written off as a contribution to the winning of the war comparable to Lend Lease or funded at low or zero rates of interest for gradual release over fifty years in the proportions 1:4:8. The terms of the American loan arrangements broadly followed these lines, although the actual wording, as opposed to the informal understandings of the time, avoided actual numbers. In the end, the solution fell short of these understandings. Britain's failure to achieve external convertibility in 1947, partially the result of a reversion to faith in gentlemen's agreements as favored by the Bank of England and some members of the Treasury,[9] and the difficulties surrounding Indian

---

[9] The Bank, worried in its own way about the postwar position of London as a financial center, favored gentlemen's arrangements to formal ones. Its pressing for such a solution lay in part behind Keynes's comment cited above (p. 32).

independence and postwar Anglo-Egyptian relations, left the authorities following a policy of defensive drift that continued into the 1970s.

Keynes's contributions to official discussions of postwar external economic policy, other than those concerned with the American Loan and the finance of the transition, largely centered around the creation of the Bretton Woods institutions (the International Monetary Fund and the World Bank), a scheme for the international regulation of primary product prices, Britain's postwar commercial policy, and, naturally, after his 1916–19 experience, Allied reparations policy.[10]

Between the beginning of the war and his entry into the Treasury, Keynes had not given much thought to the shape of the postwar international economy. However, at the end of 1940, requests from both the Ministry of Information and Anthony Eden, the foreign secretary, for a statement replying to Germany's plans for a New Order in Europe led Keynes to give the issues more thought. The resulting "Proposals to Counter the German 'New Order'" provided a good indication of the shape of the various plans that followed. The "Proposals" highlighted the following principles:

1. Friendly collaboration with the United States was essential to the creation of a better postwar world, as she was the only country likely to have the means to make many plans come to fruition and as her size and wealth would make any solution that lacked American support almost unworkable.

For Keynes, this principle was after 1940 to carry with it two corollaries: (a) It was an advantage for

[10] All of the items had concerned Keynes during the interwar years. In fact, the links were so close in the case of primary products that he wrote the first draft of his postwar scheme with a copy of his 1938 British Association address "The Policy of Government Storage of Foodstuffs and Raw Materials" (*Economic Journal*, September 1938) in front of him.

Britain to initiate ambitious schemes for many facets of the postwar world, for such schemes would stimulate the Americans to develop counterproposals for international collaboration and, it was hoped, to commit themselves to such proposals. If this commitment did not come and the Americans rejected a course of active international collaboration, they would, Keynes suggested, feel obliged to support alternative British proposals for less internationalist solutions. (b) In most cases, even after putting forward a set of proposals, British negotiators would require considerable room for maneuver in the subsequent discussions, if only because one of the primary goals of any negotiations should be American collaboration.

2. Any postwar international currency arrangements should depart markedly from the *laissez-faire* practices of 1920–33 in their acceptance of exchange-control arrangements, particularly over capital movements, and their minimization of possible monetary dislocations affecting the exchange of goods on a multilateral basis.

3. Within a framework that maximized national autonomy in economic management, international measures to provide protection against wild fluctuations in employment, prices, and markets should be necessary.

4. Postwar institutional arrangements for currency and demand management should be compatible with extensive international trade and equal access for all to the markets of the world.

5. The postwar treatment of Germany should not involve starvation or unemployment as instruments for enforcing a political settlement. Britain should favor Germany's economic reconstruction and concentrate punitive or preventative measures in the political and military areas, so that Germany could resume her role of economic leadership essential for the economic health and political stability of central Europe. If Britain did

not do this, the likely result was dominance by the alternative power in the area, the Soviet Union.

6. There should be organized relief and reconstruction aid for postwar Europe.

This set of principles served Keynes well in all the subsequent discussions of postwar international economic arrangements. In the eighteen months after their original drafting, Britain produced plans for postwar currency arrangements, commodity policy, and international trade. Behind the first two plans was the pen of Keynes, while the third was the work of James Meade. At the center of the plans, in Keynes's view, were the currency arrangements, for if these did not come into being nothing else would stand a chance. In his Clearing Union, a successor to his earlier essays on currency arrangements in *Indian Currency and Finance*, the *Tract*, the *Treatise*, and *The Means to Prosperity*, Keynes was at his most ambitious. The Clearing Union went beyond his earlier attempts in its complete break with a backed note issue in favor of a clearing arrangement whose size was related to the value of international trade; in its allowance for exchange-rate alterations according to a presumptive rule (the size of one's credit or debit with the Union in relation to one's quota); in its attempt, both through the size of the Union and the rules for exchange adjustment and controls on capital movements, to shift more of the responsibility for international economic adjustment onto the surplus countries in the system rather than those in deficit;[11] and in its provisions for the finance of relief, investment, commodity stabilization, and an international police force as part of the scheme. All of this, moreover, stood clothed in the most elegant Keynesian prose, which sur-

[11] In the past deficit countries had always found the prospective exhaustion of reserves forcing domestic action before adjustment occurred elsewhere.

vived the gauntlet of interdepartmental committees with its authorship unmistakable.

Throughout the preliminary British discussions of the Clearing Union and the other postwar schemes, Keynes argued powerfully for a multilateral, liberal, internationalist solution to the problems of the international economy rather than the imperial, bilateral arrangements favored by others. He remained skeptical, however, of merely doctrinaire principles, wherever they emerged, frequently getting himself into hot water with some of his colleagues (as he did with the Americans) as a result. Throughout, Keynes made it clear that the extent of his concessions to liberal multilateralism, especially on trade policy, depended almost entirely on the arrangements made to solve Britain's international financial problems during the transition from war to peace. Without an adequate solution to these, Britain would be unable, after the losses of the war, to take the risks of an international economy organized on liberal lines.

Eventually, of course, the plans went to the Americans. Lengthy international negotiations followed on these and less ambitious American proposals, in the course of which the British proposals disappeared while the American ones gained the safeguards to national autonomy which Keynes considered essential in the postwar world. Between bouts of negotiating with the Americans, there invariably followed periods of delay to allow ministers to give their blessing to progress so far. On the British side, these gaps usually found Keynes and others who supported his postwar vision forced to reargue their case for liberal, multilateral arrangements in place of the bilateral, sterling-area-based schemes favored by some Treasury officials, several ministers, and the Bank of England. The further the international negotiations proceeded, the more grueling the intervals became, as those who opposed the growing consensus realized that they had fewer opportunities to prevent its institutional realization. Thus between December 1943 and May 1944 Keynes was continuously involved in discussions of the draft arrangements that eventually became the International Monetary Fund. At one stage, he conveyed the situation to an indisposed colleague thus:

> It is absolutely impossible to keep you up to date with the comings and goings here, it has been a complete bedlam, which only Hoppy's [Sir Richard Hopkins'] calm hand keeps in any sort of order. Ministers are in perpetual session, driving one another crazy with their mutual ravings, the Beaver [Lord Beaverbrook] being mainly responsible, his approach and mentality being nothing short of criminal. . . . Ministers have now left Currency for Commercial Policy and, as you may suppose, confusion is still worse compounded.

True, the upshot was the Bretton Woods Conference and an agreed plan for the fund and bank. But the results were *ad referendum*, requiring parliamentary approval, and ministers refused to start this process until the terms of the Anglo-American transitional arrangements became known. Throughout 1945 rumblings continued over the fund, the evolving commercial policy consensus, and the form of the British approach for transitional assistance. Matters came to a head in December, after the signing of the Loan agreement, when Parliament was asked to approve the Loan and the Bretton Woods agreements and give its blessing to the progress of the commercial policy conversations. Again, Keynes explained the situation in a personal letter to a colleague, this time Lord Halifax, the ambassador in Washington, with whom Keynes had been closely involved in almost three months of simultaneously negotiating with the Americans and Whitehall:

The ignorance was all-embracing. So far as the public was concerned, no-one had been at any pains to explain, far less defend, what had been done. And as for the insiders, so dense a fog screen had been created that such as the Chancellor and the Governor of the Bank had only the dimmest idea of what we had given away and what we had not. . . .

However, the ignorance was not the real trouble—I suppose that it is normal among the great, and inevitable and indeed quite proper among the public. Both political parties were split on issues that had nothing to do with the technical details; and both sets of party leaders decided that a complete abdication of leadership would be the happiest way out. A section of the Socialists thought they detected too definite a smell of *laissez faire*, at any rate of anti-planning. . . .

A section of the Conservatives, led by Max [Beaverbrook] and supported by others too near to Winston [Churchill], were convinced, with some reason, that the proposed Commercial Policy ruled out Preference as a serious, substantial policy for the future; and that this, taken in conjunction with the opening of the Sterling Area, doomed the idea of an Empire economic bloc. . . .

In these circumstances, it was left to Keynes, in a reversal of his Cassandra role of the previous twenty-five years, to defend and explain official policy, in many respects the product of his drafting skill and his statesmanship, in a brilliant speech in the House of Lords on the day after his return from the negotiations.

The end of the war also brought the problem of the postwar treatment of the enemy to the fore. As noted earlier, Keynes's 1940 "Proposals" had dealt with the matter in very general terms, arguing for economic magnanimity and the rebuilding of the German economy. However, it was another year before the subject seriously began to occupy him. At first, he attempted to persuade ministers and officials to agree to provide those directly involved with planning with a series of general principles under the general rider, "Ministers should not suppose that the chief thing that matters . . . is to avoid the mistakes made last time." This attempt to stimulate discussion fell rather flat, and nothing further happened until a ministerial memorandum led to the setting up of an Interdepartmental Committee on Reparations and Economic Security (the Malkin Committee) on which Keynes was one of two Treasury representatives.

In the course of the committee's discussions during late 1942 and early 1943, Keynes clearly set out the principles which he thought should govern policy, and successfully convinced his colleagues. His first operative principle was that it should not be the function of the British Treasury to support Germany, or of Britain to provide the means, through financial assistance, of Germany's paying reparations. Given that principle, his approach distinguished between restitution, relief and occupation costs, and reparations. He saw the end of the war bringing a return of looted property, where identifiable, and a clearing up of all prewar and wartime German international financial relationships and commitments through what was effectively a declaration of Germany's international bankruptcy. During the period of occupation which would follow, which Keynes assumed would be relatively short, the first charge on Germany's output would be local occupation, relief, and reconstruction expenses. During this period, the Allies— if they did not reduce Germany's living standard below a stipulated level or impair, disproportionately to the value of the deliveries, Germany's productive capacity— could receive deliveries of stipulated goods and services in kind up to a predetermined maximum amount. Of course, the occupation, relief, and rehabilitation expenses might make such reparations deliveries completely impossible within the constraints proposed. After the occupation, Germany, which would be unable to have its own armed forces under the peace treaty and would therefore avoid the burden of defense expenditure, would contribute through an export levy to the defense and peacekeeping costs of the world, as undertaken by the great powers or an international agency, but would not pay further reparations. This framework served the committee well in its discussions and underlay its report of August 31, 1943, which Keynes used as the basis for a long talk with American officials during his autumn visit to America in 1943.

After this promising start, which could have served as the basis for British reparations policy, matters drifted. Officials continued to discuss alternative approaches to the problems, but ministers did not settle on, or even extensively discuss, the issues involved. Keynes kept up an informal interest in the work of various Treasury officials involved, but did no more, until, while in Washington for the Stage II discussions, he received from the authors a draft of the American Treasury's plan for the deindustrialization of Germany—the so-called Morgenthau Plan. There is no record of his having formally discussed the plan with Morgenthau or Harry White, but its existence, previous British ministerial neglect of the issues, and a discussion with President Roosevelt on the postwar treaty of Germany at the end of his Stage II visit filled him with foreboding. As he wrote, soon after his return to London:

> What frightens me most in the whole problem is that these issues are extremely likely to be settled by those (as I know by first-hand conversations) who have not given continuous or concentrated thought to it. . . .

. . .For, in fact, there is *no* good solution. *All* the solutions which are being talked about are, not only bad, but very bad.

No doubt, we shall refrain from making the *same mistakes* as last time. But that is not much comfort.

Despite his pessimism, Keynes retained his involvement in discussions of the problems, attempting throughout to clarify the issues, to keep Germany intact and to ask for more precise thought on the financial implications of the various proposals being canvassed. As a result, he became involved in drafting instructions on reparations for the British delegation of ministers to the Moscow conference, which was to implement the Yalta decisions—decisions which took, as usual, no account of official planning.

The results of Yalta, Potsdam, and the early stages of the military occupation of Germany left him very disheartened. When Professor Calvin Hoover wrote to him in November 1945, asking him to speak out against existing policy, as reparations deliveries were inconsistent with the Allied guarantees of a minimum standard of life for the Germans, Keynes replied on December 6:

At an earlier stage I was considerably concerned in discussions on this matter. But eventually I got to feel so hopeless about any sensible or even possible result, that I gradually disengaged myself from so distasteful a subject. Our original ideas on this matter a year or more ago were in my opinion not too bad. But, for reasons which are only too obvious, they have fallen by the way . . . and . . . only a change in policy can prevent great misfortunes.

All the same, I am afraid that this expression of opinion must remain private and personal to yourself. I can only regain complete freedom of public expression by ceasing to be officially connected with other matters. Perhaps that day may not be far off, but, at the moment, I have to behave like, at any rate, a demi-semi-official. This time I have not too bad a conscience about that, because, as I have mentioned, I am not, as I was last time, personally mixed up in responsibility for the subject. And also, because I believe that this time, both here and in the U.S.A. and also in England, the majority share my views; whereas, last time, I was a voice crying in the wilderness and had, therefore, to cry loudly.

Certainly, by that time Keynes was hoping to disengage himself gradually from his wartime level of Treasury activity. He never succeeded in doing so. Just over four months later, bitterly disappointed by the course of the first meeting of the Bretton Woods institutions, he was dead.

Conclusion

vii

Keynes himself, not to mention his influence, invariably eludes simple categories and forms of organization with his many-sidedness, his insistence on being "just 'Keynes.'" One is tempted to echo the final line of Austin Robinson's contribution to the art of short biography, which stands favorable comparison with many of Keynes's forays into the field, "Maynard Keynes was utterly unique."

Perhaps the best way to begin any conclusion on Keynes is to emphasize the continuous interplay and juxtaposition of continuity and change in everything he did. For in all his work, despite its frequent claims of modernity or even of revolution, the links to his predecessors and his early beliefs were particularly strong. Throughout there were, for example, the emphasis on the fragility of the existing social order, the concern with intelligent management as the best means of preserving that order, the "presuppositions of Harvey Road" as to the political institutions and modes of opinion-formation in Britain, and the emphasis on the individual.

The same view of the economic organization of central Europe pervaded *The Economic Consequences of the Peace* and the advice on the post-1945 treatment of Germany. The same attachment to something akin to the Fisherine tabular standard of value, taken over from Marshall, appeared in his earliest lectures, his *Tract on Monetary Reform*, his *Means to Prosperity*, and his World War II exchanges with F. A. Hayek on the ideal set of international currency arrangements. The same, broadly Marshallian modes of analysis pervade all Keynes's work, even when Marshall and his successors were the objects of attack, as in the *General Theory*.

Within this continuity—within what might largely be called, for want of a better term, a vision of a social order, its need for management, the institutions of management, and the ends of management—was continuous change. Keynes's views on the appropriate roles, methods, and goals of internal monetary management provide the best examples in this respect, for they illustrate clearly a shift from the long-run Ricardian-Marshallian view of *Indian Currency and Finance*, which emphasized institutions and essential stability, through the activist management via the short-term rate of interest of the period 1920–27, through the activist management primarily via the long-term rate of interest in 1928–32, to the interaction of long-term interest-rate management and supplementary short-term fiscal measures of the years after 1932. Each shift in emphasis was the result of the interaction of changed circumstances, new problems, and hard thought. Keynes, invariably, tried initially to meet the new circumstances and problems through old tools of analysis or minor adaptations of those tools, giving them up only when they proved unsuitable for the particular job at hand, and fashioning appropriate replacements—no more.

But what of Keynes's influence, on both the economics of his own time and that of our own? Here it is best to separate the two periods, if only because the development of various strands of economic analysis would make lumping the two· together rather misleading.

"Those of us who disagree in part with his analysis have, nevertheless, undoubtedly been affected by it in our own thinking; and it is very hard to know exactly where we stood before. Not a little of what we now believe ourselves to have known all along, it may well be we owe to him." With these words, Professor Pigou, hardly the greatest immediate admirer of Keynes's contributions to modern economics, summed up one level of his impact on his contemporaries.[1] For one influence on his contemporaries, whether they ended up agreeing with him or not, was to make them rethink their premises and reformulate their arguments, often changing them in the process. At another level, for those who were in the process of acquiring the skills of an economist at the time of publication of the *Treatise* or the *General Theory*, the emphasis was on the sense of liberation and excitement. Coupled to this was in many cases a sense of commitment to real problems, not only in the depths of the slump of the 1930s but also in 1919. Austin Robinson summed up this aspect of Keynes's influence when he remembered in 1972:

I first saw Keynes in the autumn of 1919. I had come back from trying to fly aeroplanes in the war to trying

[1] A. C. Pigou, "The Economist," in *John Maynard Keynes 1883–1946* (Cambridge, 1949), p. 22. For Pigou's moving 1949 reassessment of the *General Theory*, see his *Keynes's "General Theory": A Retrospective View* (New York, 1951).

to recover enough Latin and Greek to satisfy my college, who thought I ought to be earning my keep as a classical scholar, and finding it extremely difficult. I cut some lectures on Livy in order to go and hear Keynes give lectures on the economic consequences of the peace, and I can still picture him there in the lecture room as a young man. His burning indignation with the world, with the Treaty as it was working out, his care for the world, the sense of importance of things that he was conveying to us—these stick in my mind. Those few lectures made me decide that economics was my subject . . . and not the classics.

. . .We learnt to be professional economists—if we did—at the feet of Pigou, of Dennis Robertson and others who were absolutely first-rate teachers. But we learnt something quite quite different from Keynes— that we had got to think about the world, we had got to care about the world; that if we were going to get the problems of the world straight we had got to do it by some hard fundamental thinking. . .that if *we* were not going to think about the world nobody else was. . . .[2]

Keynes's passionate concern for the world and its ills, as we have seen, led him into most of the great economic debates of his generation. Inevitably, the atmosphere of public debate, together with Keynes's undoubted skills as a controversialist, often generated more heat than light. However, the issues and Keynes's contributions to their discussion brought to economics a generation of scholars committed to the subject for what might be called Keynesian reasons, inasmuch as they brought policy involvement to economics on a scale previously unknown.

[2] Comment in discussion at the First Keynes Seminar at Keynes College, University of Kent, appearing in D. E. Moggridge, ed., *Keynes: Aspects of the Man and his Work*, pp. 99–100.

Inevitably, some were hurt in the course of controversy with Keynes, most notably A. C. Pigou and Dennis Robertson. Pigou had felt Keynes's lash before the *General Theory* as the (unknown) chief draughtsman of the report to the Chancellor of the Exchequer recommending Britain's return to gold at prewar parity in 1925. They had, however, subsequently collaborated on the Committee of Economists of the Economic Advisory Council, on joint letters to *The Times*, and as academic colleagues. Keynes accepted that they would disagree over the *General Theory* but was distressed when Pigou's review of it spent more time taking umbrage over Keynes's carping at Marshall than in meeting the main intellectual issues. Nevertheless the feelings on both sides settled quickly. Both men had immense respect for each other, as is clear from their correspondence, and Keynes, though anxious to get his theories accepted, went to great lengths to protect Pigou's reputation. During his lifetime, Keynes failed to convince Pigou on the intellectual issues of the *General Theory* (as he failed to convince R. G. Hawtrey, despite a vast correspondence in which both took some delight), but they maintained respect for each other and friendship.

With Dennis Robertson the situation was different. If the differences between the two had been merely intellectual, then perhaps all would have been well, although Robertson's anguish over the intellectual differences he perceived was real and important. But at this stage personality came in. Robertson, a shy, diffident man, had been Keynes's pupil before 1914; they had been close collaborators in the 1920s. Keynes dated the origins of his "emancipation" from traditional theory from his discussions of Robertson's *Banking Policy and the Price Level* in 1925. In many respects, Robertson was the one person Keynes wanted to carry with him. However, Robertson, an impeccable scholar always plagued by doubts as to his own originality as an economist, deprecated Keynes's evangelism and was unsure whether he would be yielding to argument or friendship. As a result he niggled perhaps more than was necessary at the details of Keynes's vision, using these doubts as an elaborate defense of his own position and thus further straining the relationship. If matters had remained at that, relations could have continued. But they carried over into other areas of life in Cambridge and resulted in a serious break that drove Robertson to London. During the war, there was an element of reconciliation, evidenced by the two men's close collaboration over postwar international financial policy and Keynes' suggesting Robertson as Pigou's successor in the chair when he declined the honor. But elements of doubt and suspicion always remained below the surface.

The concern with policy, with the active management of the economy, meant that Keynes always emphasized the need for operational economic models. He framed his theory, whenever possible, to actually or potentially available statistics—the *Treatise* perhaps best demonstrates this process in operation. This had several important effects on contemporaries. First, they attempted to develop the relevant statistical series. The classic case here, as far as Britain is concerned, was the work on national-income accounting, which building on work by A. L. Bowley and J. C. Stamp, under the influence of the *Treatise* and the *General Theory* and wartime needs, took on its recognizable postwar form in the hands of Colin Clark, Ervin Rothbarth, Richard Stone, and James Meade. Second, Keynes's contemporaries attempted to estimate the size of the various parameters or the shapes of various relationships in the systems put up by Keynes. Perhaps the most fruitful exercise in this area was Richard Kahn's attempt to sort out the relationship between primary and secondary employment resulting from loan-financed public-works schemes suggested in *Can Lloyd George Do It?* Keynes was also fortunate in working at the time of the early development of modern econometrics, for the process of estimating and testing Keynesian relationships increased his influence among economists generally. Here one must again note that, despite his often legitimate questioning of the attitudes and methods of early econometricians, Keynes encouraged investment in such research for its practical applications. It is not all that surprising that he agreed during World War II to serve a two-year term as president of the Econometric Society. Finally, Keynes's policy orientation, along with the subsequent policy-making experience of many economists, had lasting influence on his contemporaries and modern economics in the form of attempts to link policy instruments to policy goals, not to mention a greater politicization of debate on economic issues, both in his lifetime and after.

However, if Keynes had been merely an able economist interested in questions of economic policy, his influence on his contemporaries would have hardly been sufficient to merit the attention he gained, even during the economically disturbed interwar and wartime periods. Nor would it have been sufficient to explain the radical changes in the teaching of economics that occurred between, say, 1920 and the late 1940s. For during that period, there was a marked change in the allocation of time, and space, in elementary courses and their associated textbooks among the various branches of economics. Thus, in the 1920s F. W. Taussig's *Principles* in its third edition devoted 36 of its 1147 pages to the trade cycle and 192 pages to monetary matters, while T. N. Carver's influential text devoted only 9 of its 584 pages to the trade cycle. However, in the 1940s, Lorie Tarshis's text devoted 200 of its 700 pages to national income and employment issues (excluding the foreign-trade sector), as well as 57 to money, while P. A. Samuelson's best seller, in the first of its present ten editions, devoted 126 of its 608 to the former and 75 to the latter. Surely there must have been some force behind this change, beyond the policy views and personality of Keynes, for the magnitude and speed of the change (late 1930s texts being very similar to those of the 1920s) are historically remarkable.

The change that did occur, saw a reordering of the sequence of aggregate economic analysis which proved very fruitful for economic analysis and policy-making: from the savings-dog wagging the investment-tail, to an alternative system where changes in autonomous expenditure (investment, government expenditure, and exports) affected ultimate savings through changes in the level and distribution of income via the multiplier. At the roots of this change in emphasis, as Keynes himself recognized in prefaces to later foreign editions of his *General Theory*, lay his attempt, made within the dominant English Marshallian tradition, to take monetary economics into the short period, into the real world, where different markets adjust to outside changes at different speeds under the influence of uncertainty, and where the traditional long-term analysis of a neutral money economy is irrelevant in the short term and, perhaps, misleading in the long term. It was an attempt to change the previous economics of tranquillity, or of confident foresight, into an economics of uncertainty. Keynes left economists with a series of concepts which, although they had precursors in the earlier literature, changed the way in which economists looked at the world, whether they agreed with Keynes or not. Keynes also left his contemporaries with the prospect of losing the pattern of unique, inevitable order which had characterized much of the orthodox economics of his time. Through his change in emphasis from single markets to the aggregate forms of economic behavior, he also set the stage for, and actively encouraged, attempts to understand the process of long-term economic growth— something that has proved to be a vast consumer of economist man-hours since his death.

Before I turn to the influence of Keynes on economics after his death, there is one question that I must face— why Keynes? The events of the interwar period resulted in many other attempts to shift traditional modes of analysis, as well as marginal, possibly inconsistent, accommodations of traditional theory toward new problems. The most notable of these occurred in Sweden,[3] in a school of economics following on from the Swedish equivalent of Marshall, Knut Wicksell; and in Poland, under a variety of influences, including Marx's. The economists involved, if one is to center on individuals for the purposes of classification, were Gunnar Myrdal, Eric Lindahl, and Michal Kalecki.

So then, why Keynes? Here the facile answer is that economics is (and was) a subject whose primary language is English, and that to produce interesting ideas simultaneously or a few years earlier in another language is not the best way to gain world-wide acceptance for them. But this explanation hardly accounts for the lasting impact of ideas first available in English (compare the current influence of W. S. Jevons as against that of Léon Walras, who wrote in French), and it makes very strong assumptions about economists' facility with foreign languages. No, the superiority of Keynes's formulation of relevant ideas seems to rest on other foundations: in part on their operational quality (although Kalecki's claim in this respect is also strong in the eyes

[3] The exact status of the Swedish developments, especially in terms of economic policy in Sweden, remain a subject of scholarly debate. For references see the article by B. Gustafsson, "A Perennial of Doctrinal History."

of some), in part on their ability to explain as is still clear from their dominance in elementary textbooks, the laws of motion of the economic system in a fairly straightforward way to those without an extensive training in the subject, while leaving room for later building on these basic foundations for those who want to pursue matters more deeply.

This takes us back to Keynes. Here was an applied political economist, concerned with the issues and writing in the language (words) of the civil servant wrestling with problems at hand. Yet, here also was a theorist who understood the theory he was reacting against—a theorist who trusted that "time and experience and the collaboration of a number of minds" (*JMK*, XIV, 111) would find the best way of expressing the products of his intuition. Moreover, unlike most, he took the trouble to get the argument right and worried less than most about what he had said previously.

However, not all the refinements or deeper implications of Keynes's attempt to change economists' frame of reference passed into the economics of his contemporaries. To see this, one has only to look at some of the postwar assessments of his work, one of which suggested:

> It is remarkable that so active a brain would have failed to make any contribution to economic theory; and yet except for his discussion of index numbers in Volume I of the *Treatise* and for a few remarks concerning "user cost" [in the *General Theory*], which are novel at best only in terminology and emphasis, he seems to have left no mark on pure theory.[4]

For the change in the focus of analysis reflected in the shift in the balance of early postwar textbooks found itself, from the outset, grafted onto earlier traditions.

[4] P. A. Samuelson, "The General Theory," *Econometrica*, July 1946.

The most popular graft, proved to be with the Walrasian general-equilibrium tradition, then undergoing a revival under the influence of the work of J. R. Hicks and the emigration of European scholars to England and the United States. This grafting, complete in its essentials by the early 1940s, produced a plant that appeared sufficiently robust to allow the use of Keynesian types of analysis in policy discussions and applied econometric work and in elementary undergraduate teaching, yet allowed a reconciliation between much of Keynes and the classics on the classics' own ground—the barter economy, where Keynesian uncertainty did not exist. The reasons for the success of this graft are doubtless various, but among them must surely be the strength of the earlier tradition in a world experiencing greater mathematization of the subject and the strong prevailing belief that Keynes's contribution concerned policy rather than theory, despite Keynes's protests to the contrary.

The new graft had several important effects on post-war economics. First of all, despite the *General Theory*, monetary theory and the theory of relative prices remained in their separate boxes, normally under the revised titles of macro- and microeconomics, frequently taught by different people in a university syllabus. Second, the *General Theory* became a special case within the resulting hybrid[5]—a case where wage rigidities resulting from trade-union behavior or interest-rate rigidity resulting from strongly held conventional expectations in the bond market, prevented these two prices from falling in conditions of deficient demand so as to restore the full long-term equilibrium of the system. True, economists would admit that this "disequilibrium"

[5] Joan Robinson has christened the hybrid, often called the neoclassical synthesis, the bastard Keynesian system, *Collected Economic Papers*, III (Oxford, 1965), 100. . Frank Hahn, in lectures, refers to it as "The neoclassical Bastard."

case might actually be relevant to much of real world behavior, but that did not alter its minor place in theory. Third, Keynesian economics in this form became identified with the economics of fixed prices, which left it in a weak position, after the early postwar period of straightforward excess demand, to explain price movements as a part of general economic behavior in terms other than those of excess demand or a theory of trade-union behavior formulated in the most aggregative way from casual inspection of the available statistics of wage rates, unemployment, and prices. To this neglect of price behavior was added a fourth element, a belief that in the model money largely did not matter (or did not matter very much), and that Keynesian economics primarily concerned taxation and spending policy; this belief was strengthened by early econometric work which suggested that investment was insensitive to changes in monetary policy except, perhaps, in the case of housebuilding. The stage was set, and some came to believe that inflation was a chronic problem for a monetarist counterrevolution.

This counterrevolution, associated in most minds with the work of Milton Friedman at the University of Chicago, although claiming to arise from a Chicago quantity theoretic oral tradition that carries one's mind back to the Cambridge Marshallian oral tradition of the years 1900–20, probably owed more to several of the post-1936 attempts to graft Keynes onto traditional theory and the general belief that the Keynesian revolution in economics largely concerned economic policy. The earliest exercises surrounding the monetarist revival largely centered on the statistical testing of a money-income relationship (which could be said to have its origins in the *General Theory*'s portfolio approach to the demand for money) to suggest that changes in the nominal supply of money, defined in varying ways, were the most important determinants of the level of nominal income. Added to this, in the course of the ensuing debate (which initially was badly bogged down in the discussion of the statistical results rather than theoretical matters) came an attempt to develop an analytical framework. This framework turned out on close inspection to be that of the dominant general-equilibrium tradition, shorn of its Keynesian special-case rigidities, where money mattered little in the final outcome beyond its effects on the price level—although those involved admitted that transitional periods could be difficult, especially when they involved a change from inflation to price stability or from price stability to deflation. These local difficulties aside, in the long run money was neutral, and the system tended toward "full employment" on its own. If policy-makers would only stop using the monetary system for short-term management, accept that fiscal policy was relatively unimportant in its effects on the level of demand (its main effects being to change the distribution of resources between the private and public sectors, an issue better analyzed with the tools of traditional value theory), and set some long-term monetary rule, everything would work out for the best. In some respects, this was the logical outcome of the post-Keynesian synthesis in economic theory. It produced a consistency between theoretical premises and policy advice worthy of an addition to Keynes's *General Theory* footnote compliment to Professor Robbins (*JMK*, VII, 20*n*). Such, one might say, was the outcome of the thermidor following Keynes's self-proclaimed revolution.

Recent years have seen a revival of interest on the part of economists in the types of questions raised by Keynes. The origins of this revival have been varied, ranging from dissatisfaction with the effectiveness of recent economic management to dissatisfaction with the increased formalization of economic theory along what those concerned regard as pre-Keynesian lines. The revival has taken several forms—depending on the interests, backgrounds, abilities, and intellectual proclivities of those involved.[6]

One revival, centered in Cambridge, England, but having strong Italian links, has seen early originators of and participants in the intellectual excitement surrounding the *General Theory* and their successors carry Keynes's attack on traditional theory further—into the long period ignored by the *General Theory*. Over time, this attempt has come to owe less to Keynesian constructs (Kalecki being their most useful provider of tools) than to his inspiration, as investigators have concentrated less and less on the actual short-term behavior of the system and its links to the long period and moved over to what might best be called long-term Ricardian questions.

A second revival, centered initially in the United States but of increasing interest to economists elsewhere, has a much more empirical origin. It has concerned itself with the financial implications of changing economic conditions—with the "flows of funds" that lie behind the production of goods and services recorded in the usual national income accounts. Although, as yet, this work has spawned more in the way of applied work than theoretical literature, it has sent people back to the last major theoretical works dealing with the behavior of a capitalist economy with a developed financial system: the *Treatise* and the *General Theory*. The question has also been raised again as to the implications of the financial system's responses to conditions of Keynesian uncertainty for the way contemporary eco-

[6] For a brief guide to the types of literature covered in the following general comments see the short Bibliography.

nomic theory formalizes in models the behavior of the economy.

The third revival, again broadly based over space, has its origins within the general-equilibrium system and the orthodox post-Keynesian consensus. Here, the concern—although very often buried in the pages of the more mathematically oriented of the economic journals —has been with integration of value and monetary theory. Starting from the actions of individual agents in the economic system, the traditional preoccupation of value theory, and the suggestion that Keynes's system might be dealing with disequilibrium conditions despite its rough equilibrium format, it has examined the implications of the absence of information and the existence of Keynesian uncertainty that characterize the real world for traditional general-equilibrium analysis. So far, the results, beyond leading to a revival of interest in Keynes himself rather than what post-1936 "Keynesians" said of him, have been largely negative in the sense that the inclusion of Keynes's concerns in the traditional model are highly destructive of the notion of equilibrium itself. Nevertheless, work continues along these lines to integrate the theories of value and money.

Thus one might truly say that the issues raised by Keynes, if not his particular solutions, lie at the heart of much of what contemporary economists are doing— a major accomplishment for someone who "left no mark on pure theory"! As the work progresses, it is almost inevitable that there will be future reappraisals of Keynes's work and influence.

This brief and rather loose excursion into contemporary economic research and analysis has, in some respects at least, taken us away from the real world and its problems that were Keynes's own concerns. What of his influence there? Perhaps his greatest legacy has been the general acceptance of the notion that economic management is a necessary and normal activity of governments in advanced capitalist economies. This has taken the state far beyond its earlier role of setting general guidelines and/or rules within which the economic system would operate, along with protecting and/or compensating some of those too weak to take part in or adversely affected by the working out of economic forces within those rules. It has transformed such matters as the conduct of budgetary policy, exchange-rate policy, and monetary policy, and with this altered both the activities of economists and the nature of political debate. By helping to widen the range of conceivable policy options and diminishing the acceptance of the traditional rationale of allowing the unhampered, if half-understood, working out of economic forces, it may also have increased the incidence of conflict in matters of economic policy.

Whether the effects of greater economic management have matched the hopes of the managers or their advisers is an open question. Since Keynes's death, standards have changed so much that, for example, much of the debate about whether policy actions have stabilized or destabilized various economies is beside the point. For the argument has shifted from the much larger swings of the interwar and pre-1914 periods to the consideration of relatively small swings around generally high levels of employment and output.

How much of the markedly better performance of Western economies since 1945 is itself a result of economic management rather than a long postwar investment boom, fueled by technical innovations, high levels of armaments expenditure, or some other general factor suited to the tastes of the person who is responsible for the explaining as much as to the underlying facts, is an open question. Economists just do not fully understand the process of economic growth. However, insofar as businessmen and others have believed the claims of economists and politicians that they can prevent a repetition of the large swings in output and employment of the interwar period, and insofar as this belief has affected their expectations and subsequent investment, employment, and output decisions, then Keynes's impact has been remarkable. For even an improvement in economic performance of, say, one-half of 1 per cent per annum in the level of output, taken over the period since 1945, implies a current level over one-sixth higher than would otherwise be the case. If he had done nothing else than made such an improvement possible, which is far from true, that would be a reasonable monument to the activities of one man, even if he was only an economist.

Whether this improvement in performance makes Keynes a savior of capitalism is an open question. Certainly, he had no desire to keep the system going forever. Rather, in the world as he saw it, the world of Stalin and Hitler, Keynes saw a reformed capitalism, despite its faults, as the best means of solving the economic problem—i.e., of carrying out sufficient accumulation so that society could then forget about encouraging it further in its morality, social customs, economic practices, and institutions. At that point, "the love of money as a possession . . . [would] be recognised for what it is, a somewhat disgusting morbidity, one of those semi-criminal, semi-pathological propensities which one hands over with a shudder to specialists in mental disease." The purposive man, blindly accumulating wealth as if he were a cat lover who "does not love his cat, but his cat's kittens; nor, in truth, the kittens, but only the kittens' kittens, and so on forward forever to the end of catdom" would become redundant (*JMK*, IX, 330–31).

Perhaps Keynes was naïve, or at least too much the

philosopher king, in these expectations of changing the system. But this vision of a better world dominated his activities as an economist. It was in many respects an extension of the man who delighted in the arts, good conversation, good books, close friendships—in the search for beauty and truth—and who rarely allowed the more mundane concerns of life to interfere with these more important matters. He could be arrogant, in some senses of the word, and difficult, as many anecdotes in the vast literature on Bloomsbury make clear. But in his desire to create a world where the possibilities of Bloomsbury were more widely available—both in the short term through institutions such as the London Artists Association, Camargo Ballet, Arts Theatre, and Arts Council, and in the longer term—he was prepared to devote his intuition, his intellect, his acute observation, and, in the end, his life.

APPENDIX
A Note on the Standard Presentation of the
General Theory

As Sir John Hicks's presentation of "Mr. Keynes and the Classics"[1] has entered the textbook literature of modern economics so completely, it is worth our while to look at it in the light of the discussion of the *General Theory* in this book

In the initial Hicks formulation, prices are fixed and employment is assumed to vary directly with income. The money supply is given exogenously. In equilibrium, the condition depicted by the model, savings equals investment and the demand for money equals the supply of money. Interest then centers on the relationships determining the levels of savings, investment, and the demand for money, which Hicks set out as follows:

(a) savings is a function of the level of income;

(b) investment is a function of the rate of interest;[2]

[1] *Econometrica*, April 1937. As the presentation was subsequently popularized in America by A. H. Hansen, it is often known as the Hicks-Hansen diagram.

[2] In Hicks's more general formulation, which is the common textbook version, both investment and savings are functions of *both* the rate of interest and the level of income.

(c) the demand for money is a function of the level of income and the rate of interest.

These three relationships, with the associated assumptions, allow us to derive a diagram where one curve traces the loci of combinations levels of income and rates of interest where investment is equal to savings (the IS curve) and the other traces the loci of combinations of levels of income and rates of interest where the demand for money equals the exogenously given supply of money (for Hicks the LL curve, for the textbooks the LM curve). The intersection of the two curves indicates the equilibrium solution for the system as a whole.

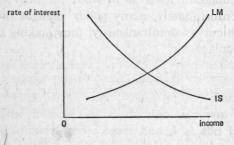

Over the past thirty-seven years this diagram has proved to be of enormous pedagogical value, for with it teachers and students can trace out the implications of differing assumptions as to the form of the underlying relationships and the effects of various policy or behavioral changes on the working of the system. Its value, however, as an accurate representation of the Keynesian system is doubtful.

Keynes himself commented on Hicks's formulation in a letter dated 31 March, 1937 (*JMK*, XIV, 79–81). In that letter he made two main points: 1) that Hicks's implicit theory of interest in the model which implied that a rise in the inducement to invest (i.e., an upward shift in the IS curve) would raise the rate of interest need not necessarily hold true; and 2) that using current income in the general formulation of the behavioral relationships overemphasized its role in the determination of expectations, especially as regards investment.[3]

The second point probably takes us to the heart of the matter. Every IS-LM diagram is in effect drawn for a given state of expectations. If a change in expectations (such as underlies a rise in the inducement to invest) causes a shift in one curve, it may also cause a shift in the other (by, say, altering liquidity preference).[4] If both curves shift, there is no clear prediction possible from the diagram itself as to what the final outcome will be. Unfortunately, many policy changes may also affect both curves simultaneously, thus making the diagram difficult to use.

One can, however, probably use the formulation reasonably safely if one talks of relatively *small* changes in the system. But if this is the case, one has to recognize that one can only draw IS-LM over that small range and not as I, and most other economists, have done over what appears to be a continuous range of values from near zero to infinity. This means that to draw the diagram properly, I must clearly indicate that only a small range of variation in the variables in the system is under consideration. To do this, I should clearly break the axes.

However, this means that the existence of an equilibrium solution for the system suggested in the normal diagram is not guaranteed. An equilibrium solution re-

[3] Sir John Hicks prints most of the letter with a commentary in his "Recollections and Documents," *Economica*, February 1973.
[4] Similarly, a rise in the supply of money, which implies a shift in the LM curve, might have such an effect on expectations that it would affect investment and, hence, the IS curve.

quires continuous curves over the whole range from zero to infinity.

Thus, although the Hicks diagram is a useful means of suggesting the implications of small changes in behavior, or in policy affecting that behavior,[5] and although it does pick up some of the differences between Keynes and his predecessors or successors in various textbook assumptions as to the shapes of the curves that result from different views of the relationships between money and goods markets, it does not pick up the full Keynesian challenge to classical theory. This is more than a matter of the shapes of particular curves. The acceptance of uncertainty *does* mean that the existence of equilibrium in the system is not guaranteed, even in so-called "special cases."

[5] For example, a change in tax policy affecting the inducement to invest.

SHORT BIBLIOGRAPHY

The standard source of Keynes's writings is *The Collected Writings of John Maynard Keynes*, edited for the Royal Economic Society by Elizabeth Johnson and Donald Moggridge and published by Macmillan and St. Martin's Press. At the time of writing, the following volumes were available:

I   *Indian Currency and Finance* (1913)
II   *The Economic Consequences of the Peace* (1919)
III   *A Revision of the Treaty* (1922)
IV   *A Tract on Monetary Reform* (1923)
V   *A Treatise on Money, 1 The Pure Theory of Money* (1930)
VI   *A Treatise on Money, 2 The Applied Theory of Money* (1930)
VII   *The General Theory of Employment, Interest and Money* (1936)
VIII   *A Treatise on Probability* (1921)
IX   *Essays in Persuasion* (1931) (full texts and additional essays)
X   *Essays in Biography* (1933) (full texts with additional biographical writings)
XIII   *The General Theory and After: Part I, Preparation*
XIV   *The General Theory and After: Part II, Defence and Development*

xv   *Activities: India and Cambridge, 1906–14*
xvi *Activities: The Treasury and Versailles, 1914–19*

In the next few years six further volumes should be available:

xvii *Activities: Treaty Revision and Reconstruction, 1920–22*

xviii *Activities: The End of Reparations, 1922–32*

and four *Activities* volumes covering Keynes's work between 1939 and 1946. Three remaining *Activities* volumes on the interwar period and three volumes of miscellaneous articles and correspondence will eventually also appear, as will the general index and bibliography.

Those without much background in economics who wish to catch the flavor of Keynes and his work could best begin with his *Essays in Persuasion* and *Essays in Biography*. The former is a collection of his attempts to mold and change public opinion and includes bits of his writings on the 1919 Versailles Peace Treaty, as well as *The Economic Consequences of Mr. Churchill, Can Lloyd George Do It? The Means to Prosperity,* and *How to Pay for the War.* The latter volume includes his biographies of Malthus, Jevons, and Marshall, his sketches of politicians at Paris in 1919, notes on friends and contemporaries, and his two papers for the Bloomsbury memoir club: "Melchior: a defeated Enemy" and "My Early Beliefs."

The literature on Keynes is vast and what follows is only a brief guide to the issues raised in this book. Readers of even a small amount of it will notice that it provides very good examples of the importance of myths in intellectual history. For the progress of Keynesian economics has been accompanied by at least two strong myths, both only now in the process of disintegration. The first, encouraged by Keynes in some of his more evangelical remarks about his predecessors and contemporaries, sees pre-1936 depression policies and policy advice as concentrating on wage cuts and rejecting countercyclical public-works policy. This myth, plus the view that Keynesian economics had nothing serious to do with economic theory, has led some revisionist authors on finding predecessors or contemporaries advocating public works (and there were many) to ask what the fuss was all about. This first myth is far from dead, as Joan Robinson and John Eatwell's recent *An Introduction to Modern Economics* (New York: McGraw Hill, 1974) indicates. The second myth accompanying the development of Keynesian economics developed during the establishment of the neoclassical synthesis. It saw Keynes in the *General Theory* simply making the special assumptions of rigid wages and a liquidity trap and thus made it possible to accommodate him as a special case in the consensus over economic theory. This myth still dominates most undergraduate textbooks.

For background to Keynes's time, as far as economic events are concerned, the best short introduction is R. S. Sayers, *A History of Economic Change in England 1880–1939* (London: Oxford University Press, 1967).

For economic thought and economic policy, especially as they concern Keynes and his ideas, see:

Davis, J. R. *The New Economics and the Old Economists.* Ames: Iowa State University Press, 1971.

Gardner, R. N. *Sterling-Dollar Diplomacy.* New York: Oxford University Press, 1956.

Horsefield, J. K. *The International Monetary Fund, 1945–1965, I Chronicles.* Washington: International Monetary Fund, 1969; Part I.

Howson, S. *Domestic Monetary Management in Britain, 1919–1938.* New York: Cambridge University Press, 1975.
———, and Winch, D. *The Economic Advisory Council, 1930–1939.* New York: Cambridge University Press, in press.

Hutchinson, T. W. *Economics and Economic Policy in Britain, 1946–1966: Some Aspects of their Inter-relations.* Clifton, N.J.: Augustus M. Kelley, 1968. (A useful, early revisionist Appendix on the 1930s in Britain.)

Mantoux, E. *The Carthaginian Peace or The Economic Consequences of Mr. Keynes.* Pittsburgh, Pa.: University of Pittsburgh Press, 1965.

Moggridge, D. E. *British Monetary Policy 1924–1931: The Norman Conquest of $4.86.* New York: Cambridge University Press, 1972.

Sayers, R. S. *Financial Policy 1939–1945.* London: H.M.S.O. and Longmans, 1956. (A superb official history of wartime policy paying much attention to Keynes's role.)

Stein, H. *The Fiscal Revolution in America.* Chicago: University of Chicago Press, 1969; esp. chapters 1–7.
Winch, D. *Economics and Policy: A Historical Study.* rev. ed. New York: International Publications Service, 1969.

The standard biography of Keynes is Sir Roy Harrod's *The Life of John Maynard Keynes* (New York: Avon, 1971). Although useful, it suffers from being too close to its subject and controversies over policy where the author's view were not always Keynes's. The best short biography is Sir Austin Robinson's "John Maynard Keynes, 1883–1946," *Economic Journal* (March 1947), reprinted with an afterword in a collection of essays edited by Robert Lekachman, mentioned below. Several other "biographical" studies of Keynes, his age, and influence exist, all heavily dependent on Harrod and Robinson for information and subject to the first myth mentioned above:

Harris, S. E. *John Maynard Keynes: Economist and Policy Maker.* New York: Charles Scribner's Sons, 1955.
Lekachman, R. *The Age of Keynes.* New York: Random House, 1966.
Stewart, M. *Keynes and After.* 1967. Reprint. Gloucester, Mass.: Peter Smith.

A most helpful and interesting collection is Milo Keynes's *Essays on John Maynard Keynes* (New York: Cambridge University Press, 1975).

The literature on Bloomsbury is vast and growing rapidly. The best short introductions with guides to the various biographies, memoirs, and studies are:

Bell, Q. *Bloomsbury.* New York: Basic Books, 1969.
Gadd, D. *The Loving Friends: A Portrait of Bloomsbury.* New York: Harcourt Brace Jovanovich, 1975.
Rosenbaum, S. P., ed. *The Bloomsbury Group: A Collection of Memoirs, Commentary and Criticism.* Toronto: University of Toronto Press, 1975.

On Keynes and the theory of probability, as well as R. M. Braithwaite's introduction to the new edition of *A Treatise on Probability* (*JMK*, VIII), see D. A. Gillies, *An Objective Theory of Probability* (New York: Barnes & Noble, 1973).

On classical monetary theory and its relation to Keynes, the best introduction is E. Eshag, *From Marshall to Keynes: An Essay on the Monetary Theory of the Cambridge School* (Clifton, N.J.: Augustus M. Kelley, 1963). For those interested in following the ideas back to their original sources, the best places to start are:

Fisher, I. *The Purchasing Power of Money.* 1911. Reprint. Clifton, N.J.: Augustus M. Kelley.
Marshall, A. *Money, Credit and Commerce.* 1923. Reprint. Clifton, N.J.: Augustus M. Kelley.
———. *Official Papers.* Ed. J. M. Keynes. London: Macmillan, 1925.
Wicksell, K. *Interest and Prices.* Trans. R. F. Kahn. London: Macmillan, 1936.

On the Cambridge didactic style see L. E. Fouraker, "The Cambridge Didactic Style," *Journal of Political Economy,* February 1958.

There are several guides to Keynes, often subject to the first myth mentioned above:

Dillard, D. *The Economics of J. M. Keynes: The Theory of a Monetary Economy.* New York: Prentice Hall, 1948.
Hansen, A. H. *A Guide to Keynes.* New York: McGraw Hill, 1953.
Klein, L. *The Keynesian Revolution.* New York: Macmillan, 1947.
Robinson, J. *Introduction to the Theory of Employment.* New York: St. Martin's Press, 1969.

For a Marxist study, see P. Mattick, *Marx and Keynes: The Limits of the Mixed Economy* (Boston: Porter Sargent, 1969).

For a provocative interpretation of Keynes's thought in the *Treatise* and *General Theory,* which links these two works to other contemporary trends in economic analysis, see G. L. S. Shackle, *The Years of High Theory: Invention and Tradition in Economic Thought 1926–1939* (New York: Cambridge University Press, 1967).

Two collections of essays on Keynesian economics are widely cited and very useful:

Harris, S. E., ed. *The New Economics: Keynes' Influence on Theory and Policy*. New York: Alfred A. Knopf, 1947.

Lekachman, R. *Keynes' General Theory: Reports of Three Decades*. New York: St. Martin's Press, 1964.

On Swedish developments in the 1930s and their subsequent effects of policy see:

Gustafsson, B. "A Perennial of Doctrinal History: Keynes and 'the Stockholm School,'" *Economy and Society*, 1973.

Lindahl, E. *Studies in the Theory of Economic Expansion*. London: Allen & Unwin, 1937.

Myrdal, G. *Monetary Equilibrium*. Trans. R. B. Bryce and W. F. Stolper. 1939. Reprint. Clifton, N.J.: Augustus M. Kelley.

The best introduction to M. Kalecki's contribution is his own *Selected Essays on the Dynamics of the Capitalist Economy* (New York: Cambridge University Press, 1971; essays 1–3).

The literature of the post-1936 neoclassical synthesis is vast. The culmination was D. Patinkin, *Money, Interest and Prices: An Integration of Monetary and Value Theory* (2d ed. New York: Harper & Row, 1964). Three influential earlier pieces were:

Hicks, J. R. "Mr. Keynes and the Classics," *Econometrica*, April 1937. Reprinted in Hicks, J. R., *Critical Essays in Monetary Theory*. Oxford: Clarendon Press, 1967.

——. *Value and Capital: An Enquiry into some Fundamental Principles of Economic Theory*. 2d ed. Oxford: Clarendon Press, 1946.

Modigliani, F. "Liquidity Preference and the Theory of Interest and Money," *Econometrica*, July 1944.

On the movements away from the neoclassical synthesis discussed in the text, the following literature is suggestive of the approaches involved:

Hahn, F. H. *On the Notion of Equilibrium in Economics*. New York: Cambridge University Press, 1973.

——, and Arrow, K. J. *General Competitive Analysis*. San Francisco: Holden-Day, 1971; chapter 14.

Kahn, R. F. *Selected Essays on Employment and Growth.* New York: Cambridge University Press, 1973. (Also includes the original multiplier article, an important extension of liquidity preference, and essays on Keynes.)

Leijonhufvud, A. *On Keynesian Economics and the Economics of Keynes: A Study in Monetary Theory.* New York: Oxford University Press, 1968.

Minsky, H. *John Maynard Keynes.* New York: Columbia University Press, 1975.

Pasinetti, L. L. *Growth and Income Distribution: Essays in Economic Theory.* New York: Cambridge University Press, 1974. (Also includes a useful essay on Keynes.)

Robinson, J. *Economic Heresies: Some Old-Fashioned Questions in Economic Theory.* New York: Basic Books, 1971.

Roe, A. R. "The Case for Flow of Funds and National Balance Sheet Accounts," *Economic Journal,* June 1973.

A useful collection of readings covering the neoclassical synthesis and the general equilibrium-based movement away from it is R. W. Clower, *Monetary Theory* (London: Penguin Books, 1969; esp. parts III and IV.)

Two provocative but unclassifiable books which deal with Keynes are:

Hicks, J. R. *The Crisis in Keynesian Economics.* New York: Basic Books, 1974.

Shackle, G. L. S. *Epistemics and Economics: A Critique of Economic Doctrines.* Cambridge: Cambridge University Press, 1972.

Those interested in my fellow editor's reaction to Keynes after her part of the *Collected Writings* might wish to consult:

Johnson, E. "The Collected Writings of John Maynard Keynes: Some Visceral Reactions." In *Essays in Modern Economics,* edited by M. Parkin and A. R. Nobay. London: Longman, 1973.

———. "John Maynard Keynes: Scientist or Politician?," *Journal of Political Economy,* January–February, 1974.

In 1972 the Univerity of Kent at Canterbury, in conjunction with Macmillan, held the first of a series of seminars on Keynes. The proceedings, entitled *Keynes: Aspects of the Man and his Work*, edited by D. E. Moggridge, appeared in 1974. A second seminar was held in 1974. The proceedings, edited by A. P. Thirwall, will appear in 1976. Future volumes should prove of considerable interest to those interested in Keynes and the impact of his work.

Since this book went to press, additional manuscript material has become available for the period of composition of the *General Theory*. This material, which alters a few minor details but not the main lines of the story told on pages 101–6, will appear as a special appendix volume to volumes XIII and XIV of the *Collected Writings of John Maynard Keynes*.

INDEX

Advisory Committee on Financial Questions, 85

American Viscose Corporation, 138–39

Apostles, 6. 7, 10, 36

Arrow, K. J., 180

"Art and the State" (1936), 40, 110

Arts Council of Great Britain, 3, 41, 118, 119n, 169

Arts Theatre, Cambridge, 2, 110, 169

Asquith, H. H., 5, 52

Attlee, Clement, 121, 133

Auden, W. H., 2

Balfour, A. J., 5, 8

Banking Policy and the Price Level (Robertson), 73, 156

Barlow, Sir Alan, 118n

bastard Keynesian system, 163n

Beaverbrook, Lord (Max), 114, 145, 146

Bekassy, Ferenc, 11

Bell, Quentin, 7n, 178

Benthamite calculus, 8

Beveridge, Sir William, 37, 127, 131, 132

Blackett, Sir Basil, 53n

Blaug, M., ix

Bloomsbury Group, 6, 7, 8, 10, 13, 36, 37, 72, 169

Bowley, A. L., 157

Braithwaite, R. B., 16, 178

Brand, R. H., 121

Bretton Woods, 103n, 142

Bridges, Sir Edward, 135

Butler, R. A., 118n

Camargo Society, 2, 169
"Cambridge didactic style,"
    30, 91, 179
Can Lloyd George Do It?
    (1929) 83, 88, 158
Carver, T. N., 158
Chamberlain, Austen, 62
Chamberlain, Neville, 114,
    123, 131
Champernowne, David,
    107
Chancellor of the Exche-
    quer's Consultative
    Council, 117, 123
Churchill, Winston, 70,
    146
Circus, the (1931), 88–90
Clark, Colin, 88, 157
Clay, Henry, 121
Clearing Union, 144–45
Clemenceau, G., 55–56
Cole, G. D. H., 122
Council for the Encour-
    agement of Music and
    the Arts, 119n
counter liquidity-
    preference, 135
Courtauld, Samuel, 138,
    139
Cox, Oscar, 118
Cunliffe Committee, 62
Cunliffe, Lord (Walter), 52

Dalton, Hugh, 136
Davies, Clement, 123
Davis, J. R., 177
Deane, P. M., ix
Dickinson, G. Lowes, 6
Dillard, D., 179
Drummond, I. M., ix

Eatwell, John, 177
Econometric Society,
    Keynes president of, 158

Economic Advisory Coun-
    cil, 82, 88, 102, 156;
    Committee on Economic
    Information, 102, 111,
    114, 116, 121n
*Economic Consequences of
    Mr. Churchill, The*
    (1925), 26, 70–71
*Economic Consequences of
    the Peace, The,* (1919),
    1, 13, 26, 54–59, 64, 153
Economic Journal, 23–24,
    26, 27–28, 88, 116, 117
"Economic Possibilities for
    Our Grandchildren"
    (1930), 40, 133, 168
Eden, Anthony, 142
effective demand, 99
Eliot, T. S., 35, 131
equilibrium at less than
    full employment, 90, 100
Eshag, E., 76n, 179
Essays in Biography
    (1933), 27, 104

Fabian Society, 122
Feinstein, C. H., 124n
"finance," 121
Finetti, Bruno de, 17
Fisher, Irving, 44–45, 46n,
    179
flow of funds analysis,
    165–66
Formal Logic (J. N.
    Keynes), 6
Forster, E. M., 7
Fouraker, L. E., 179
Friedman, Milton, 38, 163
functional finance, 24

Gadd, D., 178
Gardner, R. N., 177

Garnett, David, 11, 12, 13*n*

general equilibrium, 43, 108, 162, 166

General Theory of Employment, Interest and Money, The (1963), 1, 23, 25, 27, 28, 74, 78, 90, 91–110, 111, 113, 114, 116, 127, 135, 136, 154, 157, 161–63, 164, 165; and IS-LM framework, 171–74; and Keynes's policy advice, 102–104, 105, 107, 111–115; breaks with the past, 92–95; building blocks, 95–99; reaction to amongst economics profession, 109–10; relation to the *Treatise*, 88–90, 92, 94, 98*n*, 99, 100; reviews of, 107–109

Germany: post-1918 treatment of, 54–59; post-1945 treatment of, 59, 143–44, 147–51

Gillies, D. A., 178

Grant, Duncan, 12

Gustafsson, B., 160*n*, 180

Hahn, F. H., 163*n*, 180

Halifax, Lord (Edward), 146

Hankey, Sir Maurice, 54*n*

Hansen, A. H., 108, 171*n*, 179

Harris, S. E., 178, 180

Harrod, Sir Roy (Forbes), 13*n*, 18*n*, 21, 33*n*, 60*n*, 72*n*, 94, 100, 107, 178

Hawtrey, R. G., 63, 65–66, 107, 156

Hayek, F. A. von, 29–30, 38, 39, 88, 89, 130, 153

Henderson, H. D., 83, 103*n*, 108, 121, 131

Hicks, J. R., 23, 91, 108, 162, 171–74, 180, 181; discussion of "Mr. Keynes and the Classics," 171–74

Hicks-Hansen diagram, 171–74

Hitler, A., 55, 168

Hoover, Calvin, 150

Hopkins, Harry, 118

Hopkins, Sir Richard, 136, 146

Horsefield, J. K., 177

Howson, Susan, ix, x, 102*n*, 177

"How to Avoid a Slump" (1937), 112–13

How to Pay for the War (1940), 34, 121–27, 129, 130; political campaign surrounding, 121–124; proposals altered to achieve Keynes's purposes, 122–23

Hutchison, T. W., 177

Indian Currency and Finance (1913), 38, 49–51, 144, 153

Indian Monetary Arrangements, 49–50

Industrial Fluctuations (Pigou), 73

Isherwood, Christopher, 3

IS-LM framework, 171–74

Jevons, W. S., 37, 110, 160

Johnson, E., 13*n*, 176, 181

Kahn, Richard (later Lord), ix, 25, 73, 75, 88, 89, 90, 100, 106, 107, 113*n*, 157, 181
Kalecki, Michal, 160, 161, 165, 180
Keynes, Florence Ada, 6
Keynes, John Maynard:
  activities during World War I, 51–54
  advice on inflation (1920), 61–63, 64
  and cheap money, 85, 86, 103, 104, 112–113, 120, 124–25, 128, 134–36
  as a conscientious objector, 12–13
  as a Marshallian, 51, 53, 91, 95, 151
  on the nature of economics, 20–21, 22–23, 27, 30–31
  on the cash balances equation, 66–67, 75–76
  on the rate of interest, 63*n*, 79, 97–98
  on the trade cycle, 65
  economic advice during World War II:
    external finance, post-war, 142–51
    external finance, wartime, 136–42
    internal finance, post-war, 128–36
    internal finance, wartime, 121–28
    pre-war planning, 119–21
  economics as a moral science, 21–22
  exchange rate proposals (1919), 60–61
  exchange rate proposals (1922–25), 67–71
  exchange rate proposals (1931), 85–86
  importance of assumptions and premises to, 24–26
  method of publishing books, 2*n*
  on the nature of economic argument, 28–29
  presuppositions of Harvey Road, 33, 39
  rationalist outlook, 31–33, 35–36
  role of intuition, 27–30
  view of the political process, 33–34
  strategy for Anglo-American negotiations, 53–54, 142–143
  view of capitalism, 39–40, 168
  views on inflation, 58, 62–63, 67, 125–26
  views on inflation and full employment policies, 134–35
  views on post-1945 employment prospects, 129–30
Keynes, John Neville, 6, 21
Keynes, Milo, x, 178

Keynesian revolution, the, and Whitehall, 113–14, 123–24

Klein, L., 179

Laski, Harold, 122

Leijonhufvud, A., 181

Leith-Ross, Sir Frederick, 103*n*

Lekachman, R., 178, 180

lend lease, 138, 139

Lerner, Abba, 107

Levy, P., 11*n*, 13*n*

Lindahl, Eric, 160, 180

liquidity preference, 97–99, 100, 102, 104, 106, 134

Lloyd George, David, 52, 55

Locke, John, 45

London Artists Association, 169

London School of Economics, 108

Lopokova, Lydia, 72

Low, David, 105*n*

MacCarthy, Desmond, 6

Macmillan Committee on Finance and Industry, 82

Maisky, I. M., 118

Malthus, T. R., 27, 104

Mantoux, E., 177

marginal efficiency of capital, 97, 100, 106

Marshall, Alfred, 14, 17, 18, 19, 21, 22, 23, 27, 30, 31, 38, 179; cash balances approach, 44–46; legacy to successors, 43–44; theory of the rate of interest, 46; theory of the trade cycle, 46–49;

views on the tasks of economists (1907), 42–43. *See also* Keynes, John Maynard, as a Marshallian

Marshall Society, 121

Martin, Kingsley, 122

Mattik, P., 179

Maurice, F. D., 6

Marx, Karl, 160; Keynes's use of in lectures, 105–106

McKenna, Reginald, 34, 52

Meade, James, 88, 89, 90, 130, 131, 134, 144, 157

Means to Prosperity, The (1933), 103, 144, 153

Memoir (Sidgwick), 7

Meredith, H. O., 7

Mill, J. S., 47

Minsky, H., 181

Mises, Ludwig von, 38

Modigliani, F., 180

monetarist counter-revolution, 163–64

"Monetary Theory of Production, The" (1933), 101

Money, Credit and Commerce (Marshall), 44

Money (Robertson), 73*n*

Moore, G. E., 7, 8–10

Morgenthau, Henry, 139, 149

Morgenthau Plan, 149

multiplier, the, 88, 89, 96–97, 102, 103

"My Early Beliefs" (1938), 8–10, 36

Myrdal, Gunnar, 77*n*, 160, 180

National Debt Enquiry, 128, 133–36

National Gallery (London), 2

"National Self-Sufficiency" (1933), 105

neo-classical bastard, 163

neo-classical synthesis, 162–64

neo-liberalism, 38

neutrality of money, 46, 74, 94, 101, 159, 164

Newton, Isaac, 27

Niemeyer, Sir Otto, 14

Nixon, Richard M., 2

partial equilibrium, 43

Pasinetti, L. L., 181

Patinkin, D., 180

Pease, Beaumont, 31

Penrose, E. F., 118

Petty, William, 45

Phillips Curve, 24

Phillips, Sir Frederick, 103*n*, 114, 129

Pigou, A. C. (the Prof.), 17, 21, 22, 38, 45, 73, 88, 105, 108, 154, 155, 156

Political Economy Club (London), 104

Prices and Production (Hayek), 29

Principia Ethica (Moore), 7, 8

Principia Mathematica (Russell and Whitehead), 24

Principles of Economics (Marshall), 22, 30, 42, 43–44

Principles of Political Economy (Sidgwick), 7

Proctor, Dennis, 117

propensity to consume, 95–96, 99, 125; and Keynes's view of the future, 96

"Proposals to Counter the German 'New Order' " (1940), 142, 147

public works: in the *General Theory*, 100, 103, 104; in the *Treatise*, 81, 83–86, 100

Ramsey, F. P., 17

Reddaway, Brian, 107

"Relation of Home Investment to Employment, The" (Kahn), 88

reparations, 53, 57, 58–59, 82, 83, 148–49

Revision of the Treaty, A (1922), 59, 113

Road to Serfdom, The (Hayek), 39–40

Robbins, L. C., 22, 25, 129, 134, 164

Robertson, D. H., 25, 30, 73, 77, 88, 103, 112, 121*n*, 155, 156–57

Robinson, Austin, ix, 33, 88, 153, 154–55, 178

Robinson, Joan, ix, 73, 88, 90, 105, 107, 163*n*, 176, 179, 181

Roe, A. R., 181

Roosevelt, Franklin, 105*n*, 136, 149

Rosenbaum, S. P., 178

Rothbarth, Ervin, 157

Royal Ballet, 2

Russell, Bertrand, 6, 12, 24

Samuelson, P. A., 159, 161*n*

Sanger, C. P., 6
Sayers, R. S., 51*n*, 177
Schmoller, G., 43
Schumpeter, Joseph, 55
"Scope and Method of Economics" (Harrod), 21
Scope and Method of Political Economy, The (J. N. Keynes), 6
Shackle, G. L. S., 16*n*, 179, 181
Shove, Gerald, 12
Sidgwick, Henry, 7, 8, 21
Sidney-Turner, Saxon, 6
Simon, Sir John, 12, 121
Smuts, J. C., 54
Socialism versus Capitalism (Pigou), 25
"Some Economic Consequences of a Declining Population" (1937), 110
Sraffa, Piero, 73, 104
Stalin, J., 168
Stamp, Sir Josiah, 103*n*, 121, 157
Statistical Testing of Business Cycle Theories (Tinbergen), 21
Stein, H., 178
sterling balances, 140–42
Stewart, M., 178
Stone, Richard, 157
Strachey, James, 12
Strachey, Lytton, 6, 11, 12, 18
Study of Industrial Fluctuation, A (Robertson), 73*n*

Tarshis, Lorie, 158–59
Taussig, F. W., 158
term structure of interest rates, 79–80, 104, 128, 134
Theory of Unemployment, The (Pigou), 105
Thirwall, A. P., 182
Tinbergen, Jan, 16, 21, 26
Tobin, James, 110*n*
Tract on Monetary Reform, A (1923), 36, 66–68, 71, 144, 153
Trades Union Congress, 118, 122
Treatise on Money, A (1930), 27, 29, 66, 71, 73–86, 87, 144, 154, 157, 161, 165; analytical contributions, 76–77, 78–81; and Keynes's policy advice, 81–86; basic assumptions, 74–75; comparison with *A Tract on Monetary Reform*, 75, 79, 80; discussions after publication, 87–91; environment for composition, 73–74; Fundamental Equations, 76–78, 89–90; relationship to *General Theory*, 88–91, 92, 94, 98*n*, 99, 100, 104*n*
Treatise on Probability, A (1921), 14, 15–17, 19, 26
Trevelyan, G. M., 14

uncertainty, 92–94, 95, 109, 165, 166
University of Chicago, 108

Vic-Wells Ballet, 2
Viner, Jacob, 108–109

Waley, S. D., 64
Walras, Léon, 160
Wedgwood, Josiah, 132
White, Harry D., 149
Whitehead, A. N., 24
White Paper on Employment Policy (1944), 128, 130–32; Keynes's role in preparation of, 130–32

Wicksell, Knut, 79, 160, 179
Wilson, Woodrow, 55
Winant, J. G., 118
Winch, Donald, ix, 102*n*, 177
Wood, Sir Kingsley, 123
Wood, Sir Robert, 118*n*
Woolf, Leonard, 6